# The Model President

ALSO BY BRIAN TACANG

*The Misadventures of Millicent Madding: Bully-Be-Gone*

# The Model President

## Brian Tacang

HarperCollins*Publishers*

Library of Congress Cataloging-in-Publication Data
Tacang, Brian.
  The model president / Brian Tacang. — 1st ed.
    p.  cm.
  Summary: Junior inventor Millicent Madding is running for sixth grade class president
against the most popular and trendy girl in school.
  ISBN 978-0-06-073914-0 (trade bdg.) — ISBN 978-0-06-073915-7 (lib bdg.)
  [1. Inventors—Fiction. 2. Elections—Fiction. 3. Middle schools—Fiction. 4. Schools—
Fiction.]  I. Title.
PZ7.T1156Mo 2009                                                    2008013863
[Fic]—dc22                                                                CIP
                                                                          AC

Typography by Michelle Gengaro
1  2  3  4  5  6  7  8  9  10
❖
First Edition

*This book is dedicated to my mom, Kirispina*

# The Model President

People love to hate me because I'm lovely. They're just jealous because I'm beautifully beautiful and fashionably fashionable and . . . and . . . and they're not. Who cares that I used to have a beard? Oh. Did I say that out loud?

Pretty Liddy, the Toast of Pinnimuk City

# Prologue

**M**illicent didn't know that the rigid underpants she'd just discovered in the attic would change her life, even if only for an instant. All she knew at that moment was that they were the strangest, firmest-looking undies she'd ever seen.

Millicent moved a stack of cardboard boxes aside and held the odd undergarment up to the morning light that streamed in through the attic window. She pulled hard on it widthwise and it stretched as much as a big rubber band might.

She assumed the underwear was for ladies since the reinforced panels in the front and back had little flower motifs woven into them. It seemed as if it'd be uncomfortable, especially since it had leg extensions with little straps on the ends. At the ends of the straps were metal loops, as if they were supposed to be attached to something, though Millicent couldn't imagine what one would clip on the ends of ones' undies. The straps weren't long enough to attach the loops to ones' shoes. *Besides*, she wondered, *why would you fasten your shoes to your underwear?*

Millicent had invented a number of things over the past few years, from the Toothbrusher Ball (a motorized rubber ball with bristles that brushed your teeth automatically by rolling around in your mouth) to Bully-Be-Gone (a bully repellant that did exactly the opposite and that she'd like to forget she'd ever created). But her inventions always made sense. The same could not be said of the garment in her hands.

"Who invented this and why would a lady wear it?" she asked herself out loud. Her curiosity demanded that she trace the origins of every interesting thing. All objects, especially functional ones, had their starts with a who, what, where, or why.

"The answer to the second question is: to keep her jiggly parts from doing the rumba when she moves," Aunt Felicity said.

Millicent hadn't heard her aunt come into the attic. She gasped and let the underwear snap back to its original shape. "You startled me," she said.

"It's called a girdle," Aunt Felicity said. "Years ago women wore them to maintain shapely figures." She grabbed her fleshy hips and shook them. "I wore that very one back in my human cannonball days." She took the girdle from Millicent and admired it as if it were an old family photo.

Millicent regarded the uncomfortable-looking underwear. "You did your act in a girdle?" she asked.

"Come, now, dear," Aunt Felicity said. "You've seen pictures of me from my circus days. I wore a custom-designed polka-dotted leotard."

"That's right," Millicent said.

"I wore the girdle underneath the leotard," Aunt Felicity continued. "One can't be zooming through the air with one's fanny a-flutter. Anyway, my girdle days are gone, as are my leotard days." She folded the underwear, then turned to Millicent. "Speaking of leotards, have you found the human cannonball outfit?"

Millicent wanted to ask so many questions about the girdle as she watched Aunt Felicity return it to a cardboard box, but she decided not to. "Not yet, Aunt Felicity. I haven't made much progress cleaning up in here."

"Distracted by my old personals."

Millicent blushed.

"Wait—I thought you left your human cannonball outfit behind when . . . when you had amnesia," Millicent said a moment later. She didn't know whether or not her aunt wanted to be reminded of her memory loss. After all, Aunt Felicity had only returned less than two months ago and she'd barely talked about the many years she'd spent away from home, wandering the streets of the nearest metropolis, Pinnimuk City. Perhaps she didn't want to be reminded of her hard life as a homeless person. "I mean, I guess it's none of my business."

Aunt Felicity smiled. Millicent smiled in return, relieved.

"I left my human cannonball outfit at Ed's Balloonist Dude Ranch, where I lived for a time," Aunt Felicity said.

*A balloonist dude ranch?* The notion of her aunt living near hot air balloons—one of the best yet simplest inventions ever—was too thrilling. She scooted a box closer and rested her arm on it. "Really?"

"Really," Aunt Felicity said.

Much to Millicent's delight, her aunt launched into her amnesia story, starting with the day she'd been shot from her cannon. Something had gone awry and she'd been catapulted farther than usual. She went so far past her landing net, in fact, that she tore through the circus tent's top and went sailing high above Pinnimuk City, where the circus had been playing. Fortunately, or unfortunately, as it were, it was the day of Pinnimuk City's annual Hot Air Balloon Fiesta. Hundreds of balloons jostled for position in the sky. She landed in the basket of one of them, but she hit her head in the process, was knocked unconscious, and lost her memory. The pilot's name, she later learned, was Ed of Ed's Balloonist Dude Ranch. As she said earlier, she lived on the ranch for a time. She tended Ed's small farm and helped him conduct rides and training. Her favorite job was to assist Ed with the inflation process. "I loved being surrounded by color. Fire and color," she said. As much as she liked her responsibilities, she was restless to find out who she was and where she was from. One day, she had decided to leave to see if she could find and remember home. "There's nothing like forgetting where you're from," Aunt Felicity said. After a long silence she added, "Anyway, I'm home now, thanks to you. What were we talking about a minute ago?"

"Your costume."

"Ah, yes. A performer always keeps a spare costume or two," Aunt Felicity said. "The circus sent Phineas my extra costume after I disappeared. He said he put it here somewhere."

Though she tried to stop it, Millicent's mind wandered back to the girdle. Having another female in the house was still brand new.

Prior to Felicity's homecoming, Uncle Phineas had been

Millicent's sole guardian. Her parents, also inventors, had disappeared in a time machine they'd invented when she was much younger, so her exposure to femininities had been nonexistent. To Millicent, her aunt's behavior was a mystery. Aunt Felicity took a keen interest in "prettifying herself," as she put it. She wore makeup, and lots of it; she dusted herself with flowery-smelling powder; she painted her nails in shocking colors; and she had an evening facial ritual that included a yellow paste and cucumber slices. Aunt Felicity said that when she was homeless she'd forgotten how glamorous she was as a human cannonball. "Now," she said with a giggle, "I'm overcompensating." Millicent watched her go through her cosmetic routines in amazement. The girdle simply added to the enigma that was Aunt Felicity.

They spent the next few hours opening boxes, sorting out the usable from the useless for tomorrow's garage sale. Besides boxes of old clothes, papers, and toys, there were plenty of prototypes of Uncle Phineas's old inventions, like the Table Napkin Folder, a programmable device that was supposed to fold napkins into swans, triangles, and flowers. Millicent told Aunt Felicity that Uncle Phineas could never get it to manipulate napkins into anything other than shapes that looked vaguely like pterodactyls.

"I guess the demand for prehistoric terrors on the

dining table is rather slim," Aunt Felicity said. "But you never know—it may sell. There just might be a dinosaur-themed dinner party in someone's future." She set the apparatus aside in a pile with some other things and sighed. "We sure could use the extra money."

Millicent bit her lower lip. Uncle Phineas's inventions hadn't been selling well lately. Uncle Phineas, Aunt Felicity, and Millicent did their best to budget themselves, forgoing little pleasures like dining out at Luann's Edible Chicken Sculpture Café, which served chicken croquettes shaped like famous sculptures. To Millicent, all the entrées looked alike—from the *Venus di Milo* to the *Thinker*—but she didn't mind. She enjoyed going out to dinner.

Aunt Felicity ripped open a dusty cardboard box. "Oh!" she exclaimed. "Here it is!"

Millicent leaned in to see what Aunt Felicity had found. There, lying on a heap of clothes, was a bundle of colors, bits of sparkles, and folds of leather.

"My human cannonball costume!" Aunt Felicity exclaimed. She lifted it from the box and shook it out.

Millicent gasped. The pictures of her aunt hadn't done it justice. She'd never seen anything so outrageous yet sublime. The costume seemed to be made of both dreams and reality. Whoever wore it, she thought, would be a celebrity.

# One

Sunday morning after breakfast, Millicent tried as hard as she could to write her presidential campaign speech, but the words seemed to fall across the sheet of paper like Pick Up sticks: in no particular order and hopelessly stacked.

"What makes me think I can be class president if I can't even organize my thoughts?" she asked herself.

With a huff, she scrunched up her latest effort and threw it in the wastepaper basket. Then she stood up and stretched. Usually, her best ideas came to her in the basement laboratory, so she'd decided to try to write her speech there; but, so far, the location hadn't been of any assistance.

"I need help," she said.

She stuck her pen behind her ear and walked over to the Millennium Travel Cube, the time machine her parents, Adair and Astrid Madding, had invented. As big as a small car and as black as a witch's cap, it sat in the corner of the lab. It had lights on top and a door in the center. Above the door the words MILLENNIUM TRAVEL CUBE were engraved in silver letters. Standing before the machine, Millicent remembered the day they went into it. "Time travel, the wave of the future," her mom had said. She'd grinned her famously infectious grin, then turned to go in, her straight brown hair spinning after her. "We'll be back shortly," her father had said, bobbing his head, his curly red hair bouncing. Once inside, they had looked back at her, their heads pressed together forming a heart shape. "Bye, sweetie," they'd said in unison. Then the heavy black door had whooshed shut and they were never seen again. Looking back, Millicent wished she had taken hold of both their arms or had grabbed their white lab coats so tightly her hands would have turned blue and she would never have let go. She would have begged them not to leave. She would have bargained with them. She would have cried. *But then,* she thought, *only a time machine could have predicted it.*

Several years ago, she'd taped a picture of her mom and dad to the door. Over time, she'd taken to talking to the picture as if it were really her mother and father, which made her feel as though they hadn't disappeared in the time machine in the first place.

"Mom and Dad," she said to their photograph. The picture stared back at her, silent. "I'm having a hard time with my candidacy speech." She imagined her parents nodding as if to say "Go on." She continued, almost bashfully, "You see, I'm running for class president."

"Oh!" she imagined her mother exclaiming. "Splendid."

"What a leap forward," she made believe her father said. "I am so proud of you."

"Thanks, Dad," she answered. If she turned her head the right way and squinted just so, she could picture her parents moving—as if the photo had come to life.

"I must admit," her mother said, "I am a tad surprised. It's so civic. I've always thought of you as private."

"I am, pretty much," Millicent said. "But the other day during a student assembly, our principal, Mr. Pennystacker, asked who would be interested in running for sixth grade class president. Nobody volunteered. So Leon Finklebaum grabbed me by the elbow and thrust my hand upward."

"Is this the same Leon Finklebaum who barely stays awake?" her mother asked.

Millicent nodded. Leon Finklebaum was her math-whiz friend and a member of the Wunderkind Club, a group of the smartest and most talented kids at her school. He'd often doze off and dream about numbers.

"Awake at the one time a nap would've been handy, I'm guessing," her father said.

"At first, it bugged me that he'd volunteered me like that," Millicent agreed, "but afterward he said he did it because he knew I wouldn't have done it myself."

"Astute boy," her father said.

"He also said—" She stopped. She felt her cheeks flush. "He said I had a lot to offer as class president—I'm clever, I'm determined, and I'm persuasive—and that, maybe, all I needed was a position that asked more of me than I thought I could give." She looked at the ceiling quizzically. "I think I know what he meant."

Her mother scratched her chin. "Quite a young man," she said.

"Leon's okay," Millicent said. She avoided her parents' gaze because, for some inexplicable reason, talking about Leon made her forehead sweat. She walked back to the table where her notebook lay. "Anyway, the more I thought about it, the more I liked the idea. Now I want it more than anything."

"Terrific," her father said. "There's nothing like desire to fulfill your dreams."

"Yes, but here I am, running for class president,

against no one, with nothing to say. Pretty pathetic, huh?"

"Not at all," her mother said. "You should treat the election as though you had the toughest opponent around, and I'm sure you have plenty to say for yourself. Besides, someone may enter the fray at the last minute."

Millicent paused. She hadn't thought about another person entering the presidential race. Her heart started to thump as if she had a wild rabbit hopping back and forth in her rib cage. Her mind raced from possibility to possibility. What if Dory Splytt, the head cheerleader, decided to run for president? Or what if Jack Spunjnick, the football player, decided to run for president? Or what if Tracy Pheme, Winifred T. Langley Middle School's best actress, who could cry real tears on command, decided she wanted to be president? Dory or Jack or Tracy or any number of students at school could probably beat Millicent in a presidential race. She suddenly felt sick to her stomach and wished she had fought back harder when Leon had raised her hand for her.

"Remind me—what was the first part of what you said?" Millicent asked her mother.

"You should treat the election as though you had the toughest opponent around," her mother repeated, her eyebrow arched.

"Uh, oh, yeah," was all Millicent managed to stutter.

"Let's get started," her father said.

For the next hour, the three of them worked on Millicent's speech, building sentences and knocking them down until they got the words just right. They made sure to play up how her work ethic and problem-solving skills as an inventor lent themselves to the position of class president. They also made mention of some of Millicent's ideas, like drawing up a student body constitution, modeled after the Masonville City Constitution, which began with, "We the People of Masonville shall leave no brick unturned," and having a livestock-and-car-wash event as a fund-raiser. The more they focused on her positive traits, the more excited she became. As soon as she put a period at the end of the last sentence, Uncle Phineas walked into the basement, his white lab coat swinging. Millicent's mother and father went silent. He positioned himself near a table and clasped his hands together excitedly.

"Guess what, dear niece," he said. He'd always called Millicent *dear niece*, but with Aunt Felicity's return from her bout with amnesia, he seemed to emphasize the term of endearment even more—as though she might forget she was dear. Today, he sounded down-right tickled. He leaned against the table, cupped his chin in his palm as if he had a secret to tell her, and smiled a broad, sparkling smile. "You'll never guess, but try. Guess. It's something that you really need. Guess." Before Millicent could take a stab at it, he continued, "It's something that won't talk and won't need any of my Maxi-Gloozit Glue." He beamed at her.

The only thing Millicent could think of that seemed to talk were her old tennis shoes. The soles had come loose and flapped like lips when she walked. She'd used Uncle Phineas's invention Maxi-Gloozit Glue to stick them back on several times. The adhesive didn't work all that well, though. The soles eventually came off again. Over time, they'd accumulated lumps of dried epoxy resin, which ended up looking like teeth.

"Guess," Uncle Phineas urged.

Millicent shrugged.

"We made enough money from the garage sale to be able to afford a number of niceties, including new shoes for you, my dear."

Millicent gasped. Perhaps the future would turn out okay after all. With the help of her parents, she had completed her candidacy speech and now she was about to get new shoes. She paused for a second and thought about how Uncle Phineas and Aunt Felicity had tightened their purse strings lately. Even though they'd made money from the garage sale, they shouldn't be spending it on shoes. Millicent sighed and said, "It's okay, Uncle Phineas. I don't need them."

He approached her with a serious squint to his eyes. "Millicent," he said, "if you are denying yourself the pleasure of new shoes simply because you are trying to be thoughtful, your gesture is appreciated but not necessary." He sat down next to her on a lab stool. "We Baldernots and Maddings are quite springy—we bounce back from anything. Don't worry. Things will be looking up soon, yes?" He patted her hand.

Millicent looked at her uncle and, for the first time, noticed he had decals on his shaved head. "What are those?"

"Diffollicle Mohawk Stickers," Uncle Phineas said. "I told you things will be looking up."

Uncle Phineas had a couple of hair inventions on the market: Diffollicle Speed Gel, a tonic that completely changed one's hair color and texture—in a matter of hours—starting at the roots, and Diffollicle Mohawk Tape, an adhesive version of the gel. Though sales had slowed in the past few months, he continued to work on updates. Every day, his hair changed.

"Look," he said, pointing at his scalp. "It's a peace sign sticker, yes? Who wouldn't want a peace sign made of hair on his head?"

"Who, indeed."

"So, you see once Diffollicle Mohawk Stickers hit the market, everyone will be clamoring for them. But for now, the Shoe Stadium is having a sale."

New shoes did sound good to Millicent. Even better, she'd have them in time for her speech on Monday. She decided that she'd wear her favorite outfit and whatever new shoes she got today for the occasion. "Okay," she said to Uncle Phineas, trying not to smile too hard. "If you say so."

Uncle Phineas, Aunt Felicity, and Millicent packed themselves into Uncle Phineas's car—a shapely old car from the fifties, which Uncle Phineas had painted aqua with yellow racing stripes—and drove off to the Shoe Stadium. When they got there, they discovered that the sale was a "buy one pair, get a third shoe free" special, a detail Aunt Felicity had somehow missed when she'd read about the sale in the newspaper. The salesman told Millicent that she had to pay full price for the fourth shoe, which amounted to half the total price of a pair. Millicent asked Uncle Phineas why the store didn't just offer the second pair at half off because no one in his or her right mind would buy just a third shoe. Uncle Phineas replied, "Free sounds more enticing than half off, yes?"

Millicent picked out a pair of hiking boots and a pair of sneakers. The salesman showed her another pair of shoes called shandals which, according to him, were "the best part of a shoe and the better part of a sandal." Millicent knew he was pitching her because, to her, a shandal looked exactly like a sandal with the addition of shoelaces and a tongue. As far as inventions went, shandals weren't the cleverest. Still, she let the salesman extol the virtues of shandals because they *were* sort of cute.

"Would you like those, too?" Uncle Phineas asked.

Millicent couldn't bring herself to spend any more of Uncle Phineas's money, so she said, "No, I'm happy. I'm especially fond of the sneakers." She looked at them again. They weren't the fancy kind with squiggly motifs or punctuations of bright colors. They were rather plain. She thought of them as potatoes for feet; mostly shapeless with some eyes for laces. Still, she liked them because they were new and didn't need glue to hold the soles on. In their own odd way, they were stylish. She clutched them close to her chest.

"Perhaps you'd like some ice cream at the Mighty Masonville Mall, then," Uncle Phineas offered.

Millicent pictured herself and Uncle Phineas enjoying their favorite cones at Benton Wren's 3,100 Flavors as they had so many times before. She'd tried almost all of the flavors there, including Kiwi Surprise (a surprise because it didn't taste like kiwi the fruit, but kiwi the bird) which she found disgusting. Recently, she'd settled on Mango-Pineapple Wren's Nest on a French toast cone as her favorite. Uncle Phineas usually got two scoops of Senora Bento-lini's Lasagna Brittle in a fusilli cup. They'd sit on a bench in the mall and people watch for at least an hour, talking about ideas they had for inventions. Those times they spent together eating ice cream were among Millicent's favorites. "I second that," she said. "Sounds like fun."

Aunt Felicity snuck up behind them. "I third that," she said.

Millicent was so startled she nearly bit her tongue. "Mmm-hmm," she mumbled.

Aunt Felicity got in between Uncle Phineas and Millicent and took them both by the crooks of their arms. "Come," she said. "To Benton Wren's." The three of them went to the register and paid for the shoes, then made their way to the mall, across the parking lot from the Shoe Stadium.

While they walked, Aunt Felicity rested her arm across Millicent's shoulders. It seemed to Millicent she applied just enough pressure to make herself known. Although Aunt Felicity was the one who'd recovered from amnesia, it was Millicent who sometimes forgot that the family that had been her and Uncle Phineas for a long time now consisted of three members.

Aunt Felicity had recovered from her amnesia and returned from Pinnimuk City because of an invention of Millicent's—a potion called Bully-Be-Gone. As its name suggested, it repelled bullies. It worked by triggering pleasant scent memories in whoever smelled it, which in turn calmed him, or her, down. Unbeknownst to Millicent, Uncle Phineas had tried the fragrance on one morning. He not only spritzed himself with the cologne version but also gave himself a good lathering with the deodorant form. And he applied it all on top of his favorite cologne, Strong Like Bull. The combination of the chemicals in Bully-Be-Gone and Strong Like Bull had turned Uncle Phineas into an exploding volcano of microscopic scent particles that were carried by the breeze to Pinnimuk City many miles away. There they landed on Aunt Felicity's face as she slept in the city's central park and woke her with the smells of her former life as a circus entertainer and of her true love, Phineas, healing her amnesia. Having had her long-lost memories returned, she made her way home to Masonville.

Uncle Phineas and Aunt Felicity stopped before the entrance to the Mighty Masonville Mall, which wasn't big, as its name implied, but moderately sized. It was named after Minnie Mighty, Masonville's shortest retailer and built on the original site of her boutique: Minnie Mighty's Mini Muumuu's. "After you," both Uncle Phineas and Aunt Felicity said to Millicent. They made their way up the escalator to Benton Wren's in the food court.

On the second floor, they passed a runway that had been dressed with a silver metallic skirt. Around its perimeter, bright spotlights stood on cranelike tripods. Large speakers anchored the head of the ramp, where a curtained cubicle created a backstage area. People shopping the mall had already started sitting in some of the chairs that flanked the runway.

The three of them stopped. Millicent was fascinated with the glistening fabric. It almost looked as if it were made of computer chips. She made a mental note to invent a computerized fabric someday.

"Whatever is this?" Uncle Phineas asked. He went up to touch the fabric skirting the stage. "Seems a setup for a show, yes? But what sort of show? Magic? Puppet?"

Millicent chuckled.

"Talent?" he added.

"A fashion show," Aunt Felicity interjected.

"Oh, I see," Uncle Phineas said. He pursed his lips. Millicent thought he looked out of his element, even confused. "No, I don't, actually," he continued. "Seems highly inefficient, yes? I mean, why would one watch someone wearing an ensemble walking down a ramp when one could easily go into a store to see the very same outfit on a hanger? No middleman . . . -woman . . . person."

Aunt Felicity slipped her hand into the crook of Phineas's arm. "You were never one for fluff," she said.

"I can learn to enjoy frivolities," Phineas said. He paused, then shook his head. "No, you're right. Not my thing." He looked at Millicent. She'd been eyeing the setup. "Why don't you watch the show," he said, "and we'll go and get you your favorite ice cream. What do you say?"

"Okay," she said. Although she thought of herself as the least trendy of her group of friends, she did find clothes interesting when viewed as inventions. The fact that designers could come up with so many variations of sleeves and pant legs seemed nearly ingenious. She had once considered creating a suit that could do something spectacular, but what, she didn't know. And how she'd make it she *really* didn't know. Still, the show might give her enough inspiration to learn clothing construction skills.

"I'll be sitting near the front," she called out to her aunt and uncle as they sauntered toward the food court.

She slipped into a chair in the second row behind a woman in an overlarge hat, then scooted down two seats because she couldn't see past the hat to the runway. Seconds later, a girl about her age shimmied up a set of steps and onto the stage. The girl shook her glistening black hair, which emphasized that the tips were dyed hot pink. She shifted her charcoal-colored velvet skirt and adjusted her shiny, red jacket. Millicent scanned the girl from her head to her perfect patent leather boots. Even Millicent could discern that the girl hadn't gotten them at the Shoe Stadium.

In spite of her fashionable outfit, the girl's face seemed to command everyone's attention. Her makeup had been done with artistic precision, each plane and line dusted or drawn as if it were done by Masonville's most famous painter, Ludwig the Realist, onto an already perfect face.

Millicent felt a tickle in her stomach. If she didn't know any better, she would have thought it was a pang of jealousy. She looked at the girl's flawlessly outlined heart-shaped lips. Uncle Phineas didn't allow her to wear makeup. Her stomach zinged her again. *Maybe I'm just hungry*, she thought.

The girl tapped the microphone. "Hello," she said. "My name is Ebi Sato. On behalf of Pretty Liddy's Junior

Fashion Academy, I welcome you to our fashion show called Fabulous Fall Fashion's Fabulisticness . . . for Fall." She scrunched up her eyes and nose as if she didn't understand what she'd just said.

Millicent had heard of Pretty Liddy's Junior Fashion Academy. The school taught young models, designers, photographers, and others whose futures were to be sewn up in the glamorous world of high fashion. The students were often seen sashaying and parading around town in the latest styles—some styles so current they couldn't even be found in stores. And by the time those fashions showed up a year later in the Mighty Masonville Mall, the Pretty Liddys were into different looks altogether.

"Today's show features clothes from some of our favorite mall boutiques, including Excruciating Mark-Ups and Ten-Minute Trends," Ebi said. "We will close with a special announcement. But before that we'll show an original design by Pretty Liddy's Junior Fashion Academy's own designer of tomorrow, Paisley Slub, to be worn by one of our pretty models."

"Our *most beautiful* model," a girl said from behind the curtains.

"Most beautiful."

"Most *gorgeous*."

Ebi squirmed a little as she echoed, "Most gorgeous."

"Voted this year's *Fad* magazine's Little Supermodel," the voice said.

Ebi curled her lips, then said through her teeth, "Voted *Fad* magazine's Super Little Model."

"Little Super, dingbat."

"You were voted *Fad* magazine's Little Super Dingbat?" Ebi asked.

"Give me that," the girl behind the curtain barked. Ebi shoved the microphone backstage. "I'm Fiona Dimmet and I was voted *Fad* magazine's LITTLE SUPER-MODEL," the girl said.

The crowd oohed and aahed.

Millicent knew about Fiona Dimmet's accomplishments because one couldn't live in Masonville without seeing Fiona's face or hearing her name. When Fiona was seven, she'd been chosen to be Young Miss Mortar and had led the annual Big Brick Parade, which celebrated the town's status as Home of the Really Big Brick. By ten years of age, she'd won several beauty pageant titles, including Miss Teeth-So-Luminous, Mini Miss Manicured, and Ultimate Miss Hair-O-Plenty. Recently, she'd been featured in numerous department store catalogs and newspaper ads. She was so well known that many people stopped referring to her by her full name and simply called her Fiona. And she was as gorgeous as she claimed to be. Just knowing Fiona would be walking by her made Millicent feel awkward and rickety like a marionette.

Dance music started up, banging and chinging so loudly Millicent felt it in her metal chair. By then, Ebi had taken back the microphone long enough to shout into it, "Fabulous Fall Fashion's Fabulisticness . . . for Fall!"

A boy with spiked platinum blond hair, dressed entirely in black, ran to the head of the runway, a flash camera in hand. He skidded to a stop, his bright green sneakers screeching on the tile floor, and began snapping pictures of the first model to strut the stage. "Superberific," he muttered.

Millicent wished she had a pocket dictionary on her to give the boy. But she quickly shifted her focus from him to the colorful clothing whizzing past. She found the outfits amusing and slightly desirable. She even entertained the thought of what it would be like to wear one of them. The kids were some of the nicest looking she'd ever seen. And none of the girls she knew wore makeup so well, if they wore makeup at all. The combination of the music, the fancy clothes, and the pretty models made the whole event feel dreamlike. Before she knew it, the show came to a close, except the final ensemble.

The music changed to a song with heavy percussion and the lights intensified. Out came the beautiful Fiona Dimmet, her long, blond hair flying. Her eyelids were smudged with a smoky color and her cheeks were dashed with blush. Her lips smoldered as red as a smart remark. She wore what Millicent thought of as a fabric contraption—an impractical tangle of sleeves and fuzziness. As useless a garment as she thought it was, Millicent still liked it. Fiona marched down the runway. The entire mall seemed to fall silent as all eyes focused on her. She did a dramatic twirl, then started to tromp back toward the curtains.

Some people in the audience applauded.

Suddenly Fiona's eyes landed on Millicent. She did a double take, then stopped in her tracks. The clapping quieted. "Oh, call the fashion paramedics," she said to Millicent. "You need that shirt amputated from those pants. Just because they both fit you doesn't mean they go together." She threw her head back and laughed as she finished her walk.

For a second, Millicent hoped that no one had heard Fiona, but the gales of laughter that surrounded her proved otherwise. A contracting sensation in her chest tugged her downward until she couldn't help but slump in her chair. Her ears throbbed and she felt the blood drain from her cheeks.

*Where are Uncle Phineas and Aunt Felicity?*

She fought back tears, hoping for something to distract the people staring at her. Nothing and no one came to her rescue for what seemed like minutes.

Just then, Ebi returned to the microphone with another girl in tow, and the audience slowly turned to face the stage. The girl had pale skin and straight hair the color of a cardboard box.

"Our photographer for this event was Heinrich Putzkammer," Ebi said. "Heinrich, take a bow." The boy who'd been taking pictures and muttering "superberific" bowed his spiky head. "And this is Paisley Slub," Ebi continued, "the designer of our last outfit."

Paisley bowed so low her hair fell in front of her face.

"We have one final announcement," Ebi said. "On Monday, Pretty Liddy's Junior Fashion Academy will be closed for major renovations—something about termites. Those are bugs that eat wood, right?"

"Right," the lady in the big hat said.

"We looked a long time for a school that had some extra rooms we could use to hold classes. But we couldn't find any schools that would take us. It was sad."

*Poor fashionistas*, Millicent thought. The blood had started to return to her head and she felt her nerve return, too.

"But then we found a middle school," Ebi said. "I forgot the name of it. It's a funny, lady's name. What's the name, again?" she asked the lady in the big hat.

Millicent's blood drained back down from her cheeks. She riffled through the names of middle schools in Masonville. *Let's see*, she thought, *there's Eli Histrionica's School of Performing Arts and Masonville Middle, but those aren't named after ladies. . . .*

The woman in the hat got up, went to the edge of the stage, and beckoned Ebi over to her. She whispered something in Ebi's ear.

*Then there's Jane Thomas's School for Tweeners, but that isn't a funny name—except for the Tweener part.* Millicent tried her best to think of other middle schools in Masonville, but she could only think of one other.

Ebi returned to the microphone stand. "While we wait for our new and improved school," she said, "we'll be going to . . ."

Millicent held her breath, hoping she'd forgotten an obscure middle school with a peculiar woman's name. *Please don't say Winifred T. Langley Middle School*, she thought. If the Pretty Liddys were, by some horrible stroke of luck, to attend her school, she foresaw the worst for her and her friends in the Wunderkind Club. Fiona had embarrassed her, practically to the point of tears, in front of dozens of people, and if all the Pretty Liddys were as mean as Fiona, how would they treat the Wunderkinder? And if they were going to attend her school, she'd have to warn her friends as soon as possible.

"Winifred T. Langley Middle School," Ebi announced.

Millicent felt her blood cascade all the way down her legs where it pooled in her feet which, in turn, rested in very bad shoes.

# Two

The next morning, Millicent threw her backpack into the sport utility vehicle Uncle Phineas had given her a couple of years ago. It was olive green and had a roll bar. A small version of an adult-sized SUV, it had every amenity a real one had, except that it ran on electricity. She jumped in, started the engine, and barely closed the door before driving down the sidewalk to the Masonville public library and the Wunderkind Club's secret meeting chamber.

Millicent pulled into the library parking lot a couple of minutes later. She had called an emergency gathering of the Wunderkinder via e-mail. She'd kept its subject undisclosed because she knew her friends needed to hear her news firsthand. Tonisha, Juanita, and Pollock pestered her to tell them the purpose of the meeting, but she didn't give in. Roderick wrote back: *m, this had better be worth it.* The only Wunderkind she hadn't heard from was Leon. They begrudgingly agreed to convene half an hour before school. Millicent parked next to Miss Ogelvie's car.

She grabbed her backpack and ran to the library's main entrance. She heaved open one of the heavy glass doors, but it got the best of her and pushed her back outside. She wrested it open with a groan just as Miss Ogelvie walked past, pushing a metal cart teetering with books.

Miss Ogelvie grunted to a stop. "A little raucous this morning, aren't we, Miss Madding?" she asked. She planted her hands on her hips, her muscular biceps rippling. Miss Ogelvie had her arms tattooed with her favorite authors, and it was Amy Tan who seemed to be grimacing at Millicent that moment.

Millicent nodded breathlessly.

"Don't make a habit of noisiness," Miss Ogelvie said. She resumed pushing the cart. "Your friends are in the . . . chamber," she added, not looking at Millicent.

The chamber had been created in the mid-seventeen hundreds by Millicent's great-great-great-great grand-mother, a librarian known as Goody Constance Madding. The room lay behind a rolling bookcase and down a flight of stone steps. Goody Constance Madding had excavated it to save a collection of books the local villagers were bent on burning. Only the descendants of Goody Madding and a few others, like the Wunderkinder and Miss Ogelvie, knew of its existence.

Millicent made her way to the back of the library to the children's section and to Goody Madding's secret room. Well ahead of her time, Goody Madding had engineered a bookcase to operate on wheels, and the whole thing was activated by a hidden trigger. Millicent checked to make sure no one lingered nearby before pushing on the special brick in the wall near the fiction shelf. The bookcase creaked, then gave way, its wheels gliding as if they'd just been oiled by Goody Madding herself, to reveal the old wooden door to the underground room.

Millicent opened the door and descended the steps. Already, she could hear the Wunderkinder talking in hushed tones, and she could see the dim glow of the candelabrum that provided the room with light.

"Do you know what this is about?" Tonisha, the Wunderkind poet, asked. "Maybe it's about her presidential campaign. No, she would have told me if that's what it's about. I'm supposed to be her best friend and she didn't give me a clue. If only I had the language to convey the sense of betrayal I feel. I think I'll write a poem about it."

"The e-mail said emergency meeting. That's it," Juanita said. "Do you all mind if I practice my violin?"

Juanita always played her violin, usually without asking.

"I mind," Pollock, the Wunderkind artist, mumbled. "And don't put it on top of my portfolio. I've got a brand-new painting in there."

"All I can say is she's late," Roderick, the Wunderkind future CEO, said. "Late, late, late. If she were employed in my mother's corporation, Beauty Goo Cosmetics, or my father's law firm, Biggleton, Wigglebum, and Higglebee, she would have been fired by now."

"We know what your parents do," Tonisha said. "You tell us all the time."

"One can never tout success enough," Roderick replied.

Millicent stepped into the puddle of candlelight at the base of the steps.

"Millicent," Pollock said.

"It's about time," Roderick said.

"Is this serious?" Juanita asked.

Tonisha popped up. "What's this all about?"

Millicent scanned the group, studying her friends' clothing. Pollock wore the usual: an outfit paint splattered to the point of being indistinguishable from all his other paint-splattered clothes. His shoes were dotted with color, too. Always aspiring to be a businessman, Roderick wore dress slacks and a white, button-down shirt with a red bow tie tied so tight his face matched it. Juanita had on one of her frothy, ruffled tops, which made her look like an éclair. Her mother made them for her because she said the clothes in the stores weren't feminine enough. Tonisha had on an especially tall headwrap made of a colorful African fabric, and behind her ear she had a pencil. Looking at her friends in their quirky attire, all Millicent saw were eccentric targets the Pretty Liddys would aim for, one by one, with their rudeness.

"Well?" Tonisha asked. "What's this all about and why are you staring at us like that?"

Millicent went to the head of the long table that sat in the center of the room. She pressed her palms on it and leaned forward, making eye contact with each Wunderkind. She knew she had to get them to take her seriously, so she decided to try a selling technique she sometimes used when she introduced one of her new inventions to the Wunderkinder: instilling fear.

"There is a dark cloud of cruelty heading our way as we speak," Millicent said, "and it's made of pretty people and it rains insults." She hoped her speech sounded melodramatic enough to captivate them.

"How melodramatic," Pollock said.

*Yes!* Millicent thought.

Tonisha said, "I'm the poet around here."

"You need suspenseful background music," Juanita said. She inched her hand toward her violin.

"Don't," Roderick said to Juanita. He turned his attention to his watch, then to Millicent. "Get to the point. We're going to be late for school."

"Two words," Millicent said, "Pretty Liddy."

"Pretty Liddy? What's that?" Juanita asked.

"Okay, five words," Millicent said. "Pretty Liddy's Junior Fashion Academy."

"I've heard of that school," Tonisha said. "It's supposed to be fabulous."

"What?" Millicent blurted.

"That's right. I remember now," Juanita said. "All the coolest, most fashionable kids go there. I wish I had one of their wardrobes."

"Truer words have never been spoken," Tonisha said.

"I hear they have a good design program," Pollock said.

This wasn't going the way Millicent had hoped.

"What does Pretty Liddy's Junior Fashion Academy have to do with us?" Roderick asked impatiently.

"It's closing temporarily," Millicent answered. She waited for some kind of response, but the Wunderkinder simply stared back at her. "And the Pretty Liddys will be attending Winifred T. Langley Middle School starting TODAY."

"Oh, my gosh!" Tonisha shouted.

"Yikes!" Juanita yelled.

Now her friends were behaving as she'd expected. Of course they didn't want a bunch of fashion victims going to their school.

"Millicent! I wish you had told me sooner," Tonisha said. "I didn't even wear a belt today." She turned to Juanita. "These jeans are crying out for a belt, aren't they? Aren't they?" She slipped her thumbs into her belt loops and pulled.

"You're so smart," Juanita whined. "A belt is what this skirt needs." She glared at her waistband, then fussed with her ruffled blouse, tucking it into her skirt and pulling it out again. "What about my top? I look like a piñata, don't I?"

"No, you don't," Tonisha said. "Well, sort of. But not a big one."

Juanita huffed. "I'm going to make my mom take me shopping this afternoon. No, not my mom. She has bad taste."

"My mom will take us," Tonisha said.

"What's the big deal?" Pollock said as he licked his palm, then smoothed his hair flat. He started picking at the paint splotches on his clothes but gave up after a couple of seconds.

"I usually keep a dressy bow tie in here," Roderick said. He popped his briefcase open and rummaged through it.

"What's wrong with you people?" Millicent asked, but no one heard her.

"We've got to get out of here. We're going to be late," Roderick urged. He finished tying his tie which, to Millicent, looked an awful lot like the one for which he'd swapped it.

The Wunderkinder dashed out of the secret chamber, leaving Millicent alone with the musty books and sputtering candles.

As Millicent pulled into the parking lot of Winifred T. Langley Middle School she saw what looked like the entire student body huddled in groups on the front lawn. They were also clumped around the Winifred T. Langley Memorial Fountain, which portrayed the school's eccentric namesake—contortionist, linguist, and chef—in all her glory. Everyone appeared to be deep in conversation, occasionally looking up as if they were expecting visiting dignitaries. Mr. Pennystacker, the school principal, stood there, too, his hands clasped under his paunch, alternately twiddling his thumbs and his pinkies.

Millicent flew into her parking space.

Leon Finklebaum, the Wunderkind math whiz, scuttled toward her as she turned off her car. "Hey, Millicent, what's going on?" he called. "Sorry I missed your meeting. I overslept. Are you ready to give your speech today?"

Millicent had forgotten all about her speech. "I don't know," she said. "I practiced a little. I've been preoccupied, Leon."

"Oh."

Suddenly Roderick, Tonisha, Juanita, and Pollock ran past. Tonisha had something in her hand and was fiddling with it.

"I didn't see you guys on the way over here," Millicent called out.

"We took the short cut through Mr. Miller's field," Tonisha hollered over her shoulder.

Leon, puzzled, looked at their friends racing to the fountain. "What's up with them?"

Millicent quickly told him about how she'd been

ridiculed by Fiona Dimmet at the fashion show and how embarrassing it was to be laughed at by dozens of people and how the Pretty Liddys were going to show up any second and how they were going to be temporary students at Winifred T. Langley Middle School and how each one of the Wunderkinder was sure to experience the same ridicule she had.

"I mean, Leon, really," she said. She looked at Leon's pocket protector, which did nothing to keep his shirt from getting stained. He often poked himself accidentally with pens well beyond the borders of the protector when he tried to put them in his pocket. "They'll probably start with you," she added.

"So?"

Just then, two cars pulled up in front of the school. The first, a black van, eased to a stop. The second car, a white luxury sedan as large as a killer whale, beached itself near the curb, its tires making a cushy sound as it came to a halt. The Winifred T. Langley students lapsed into silence, craning their necks to see who would come out.

Millicent strained to see, too, but all she could make out was the silhouette of an enormous hat above the driver's seat. "Come on," she said to Leon. She grabbed him by the hand and led him to where the other

Wunderkinder stood near the fountain.

Now Millicent saw what Tonisha had in her hand—an eFone—a combination phone, computer, and compact mirror. She'd been looking up Pretty Liddy's Junior Fashion Academy online.

A bunch of stylish kids piled out of the van. Millicent recognized them from the fashion show at the mall. The Winifred T. Langley students silently watched the new kids.

After what seemed like minutes, the sedan's back door opened and out stepped a boy dressed entirely in black, except for orange leather sneakers. Millicent remembered him as the photographer from the fashion show at the mall. His spiked platinum blond hair glowed in the morning sun. He wore an expensive silver camera around his neck. With both hands, he made a square with his thumbs and forefingers as if he were envisioning a picture.

"That's Heinrich Putzkammer. He's a photographer," Tonisha said. She showed everyone his picture on her eFone. "He's divine."

"He's fabulous," Juanita said. "I love his whole look."

Millicent gawked. She couldn't believe her ears.

Next, a pretty girl in a cloud of fake fur exited the car. Millicent remembered her as the announcer from the fashion show. Her glistening black hair still had hot pink tips, and she wore a cheetah-patterned headband. Her jacket was black fake fur; her fake-fur-trimmed black-and-fuchsia tartan skirt was made of a satin so shimmery it seemed to play tricks on the eye; and even her platform shoes were covered in fake fur.

"She looks exotic," Juanita said.

"I just saw her picture. Her name is Leiko Sato," Tonisha whispered, "but she goes by Ebi. She's a make-up artist and model."

"Ebi is shrimp sushi," Pollock said, absentmindedly staring at Ebi's face.

"Be quiet," Tonisha snapped.

"I'm just saying . . ." Pollock mumbled, then went back to staring at Ebi.

Heinrich circled Ebi, his camera poised. Suddenly he boomed to her, "Give me attitude."

Ebi pouted, then flung her head back.

"That's it. Work it. Say your name—growl it like a cheetah," Heinrich said, clicking pictures of Ebi.

Ebi planted her hands on her hips and snarled, "Ebi, I'm Ebi."

"Who are you? Who is the glamouristic one? And who is the beautifulest one?" Heinrich asked as he snapped more photos of her.

"I am Ebi," she said. "The glamouristic one is Ebi and—" she peered at the car as if she might get into trouble, then added quietly "—the beautifulest one is Ebi."

"Again, closer," Heinrich said. He circled her, his movements sharklike.

Ebi twisted her torso and leaned into the camera. "The beautifulest one is Ebiiiiiii," she whispered.

Millicent stared at the commotion. *This is the most bizarre thing I've ever seen*, she thought. She glanced at all her friends, who seemed to be enthralled with the goings-on—all except Leon, who looked as if he were about to doze off.

"I wonder if Ebi's got a manager," Roderick said. "I could make her famous."

Millicent shrugged. At least Roderick sounded like his usual enterprising self.

Another girl stepped out of the car, this one with long, straight, bland-looking hair. Millicent recalled that she had designed an outfit for the mall fashion show. Millicent tried to remember her name, but she couldn't. The girl carried a portfolio under one arm and a laptop computer under the other. She wore a gauzy, ruffled, lilac top that fluttered when she moved. It looked as if she were surrounded by butterflies. She also had on avocado-green jeans with lilacs embroidered on their hems. Millicent noticed that she had pink high heels on. Millicent was not allowed to wear high heels because Uncle Phineas believed they were bad for developing feet. "Besides," Uncle Phineas had said, "you're not old enough." She found herself feeling as envious a green as the girl's jeans.

"Oh"—Tonisha sighed longingly—"that's Paisley Slub."

*That's right,* Millicent thought. *Paisley.*

"She's a designer," Tonisha continued. "She makes most of her own clothes—and some clothes for the other Pretty Liddys. I wish I had even a drop of her talent."

The Wunderkinder collectively inched forward to get a closer look.

"She's wearing Savant Jeans," Juanita gasped.

Millicent had heard of Savant Jeans. They were carried in a pricey boutique downtown called Don't Even Think About It, where the sales clerks all said, "Don't even think about it" when they saw people come into the store who looked as though they might not be able to afford the clothing there.

"Paisley," Heinrich said, his camera poised, "give me a fabulistic pout."

"Why does he keep making up words?" Millicent asked. His language mangling made her itchy, so she scratched her neck. Tonisha and Juanita both shushed her. She frowned at Tonisha, the poet, who, of all the Wunderkinder, should have been irritated.

Paisley went red in the cheeks and she let her hair fall in front of her face. "Heinrich? You know I don't like my picture taken?" she said in a mousy voice.

"Just one pose," Heinrich said.

Paisley dropped her shoulders and rolled her eyes. "Heinrich, no?"

Millicent whispered to Tonisha, "Her voice goes up at the ends of her sentences. It makes everything she says sound like a question."

"It's called upward inflection," Tonisha whispered back. "People with low self-esteem tend to do that."

Millicent muttered, "Ooooh, I see." But Paisley seemed to have every reason to feel good about herself. She had beauty, style, and evidently loads of talent going for her. *Why,* Millicent thought, *would she be lacking in self-esteem?*

"I can tell I must show you how to pose," Heinrich continued. He set his camera down. Then, without warning, he went into a rapid succession of painful-looking poses, some of which were almost worthy of the contortionist Winifred T. Langley herself.

"Oh, my goodness, is he okay?" Tonisha asked.

"Someone get the school nurse," Juanita urged.

"Quiet!" Ebi shouted at the gasping crowd.

"What is he doing?" Pollock asked.

Ebi shuffled toward the Wunderkinder as quickly as her platform shoes would allow. "He is doing the Heinrich maneuver—searching for a never-before-photographed pose. He must have complete concentration." She pressed both her forefingers to her temples to emphasize her point.

Heinrich stopped with his back arched, his left hand touching the concrete, his right hand reaching for the sky. "This. This is what I want, Paisley. Spectabulous."

"Heinrich, I'm not doing that? I'm just a designer," Paisley said.

A hand reached out of the white sedan and pushed Paisley aside. "I'll do it," a girl's voice growled. "You're hopeless."

All eyes turned toward the car.

# Three

Murmurs rippled through the crowd as a turquoise patent-leather boot with a toe as pointed as a fingernail landed on the sidewalk. Millicent clutched her backpack over her chest in an attempt to cover her outfit and crossed her feet, pigeon-toed, to hide her shoes. She pulled at her rough, plaid wool shirt jacket, wondering if shirt jackets were in style, much less plaid ones.

Her friends had lurched in front of her so that they could see Fiona Dimmet. Millicent peeked between Tonisha and Juanita.

"Oh," Juanita sighed.

"Those boots are so fab, they deserve their own haiku," Tonisha said. She whipped out her poetry journal, pulled the pencil from behind her ear, and started scribbling.

*Fab?* Millicent thought.

The student body went silent in anticipation. In a

move as graceful as an egret's, Fiona Dimmet sprang from the car and stood before her rapt audience. She whipped her head about, her glossy blond hair cascading around her.

"Her hair is like a Thoroughbred horse's mane," Tonisha said.

"And her outfit is scrumptious," Juanita said.

"She's pretty," Roderick gasped.

Millicent had to admit to herself that Fiona's ensemble did make her mouth water a bit. Fiona had on a plum-colored jacket with lime green and turquoise printed medallions on it. Her yellow skirt featured a wide belt with a big turquoise buckle. Millicent thought she could never carry off such a bold look, much less even know how to put such an outfit together, which only made her more envious. "She's colorful. I'll give her that."

Tonisha elbowed her.

Fiona surveyed the school's facade. "So, this is Winifred T. Langley," she blurted. "What does the T. stand for? Trashed?" She let out a laugh and, except for Paisley, the other Pretty Liddys echoed her.

"Or tired." Heinrich giggled.

"Or tragic," said Ebi.

"I think it's kind of charming?" Paisley said. "I like

the—" Fiona shot her a glare. "Fountain," she added quietly.

"Don't you have some hemming to do?" Fiona barked.

"Right," Paisley answered.

Mr. Pennystacker approached the Pretty Liddys like an old, lopsided cart, his chest heaving and his shoes squeaking. "I'm Principal Pennystacker. Welcome to Winifred T. Langley Middle School. The 'T,' by the way, stands for Theodocia. Winifred Theodocia Langley— otherwise known as the famous contortionist the Bendable Francine Tippit—was, for a short time, due to amnesia, a chef and linguist. It is she who is depicted by this fountain." He gestured toward the metal water feature. "Here you see her in a contortionist's pose, sitting on her own head while reading a book. She lost her memory from an unfortunate fall into a tuba. That's why it features a tuba spouting water. Fascinating tidbits of historic information, wouldn't you say?"

Fiona rolled her eyes. "If you say so."

Millicent frowned. She loved the Winifred T. Langley story and fountain.

"Since you are something of a club yourselves," Mr. Pennystacker continued, "allow me to introduce you to some of the school's student organizations." He brought the Pretty Liddys around to the Three Spigoteers, a trio of kids who had a thing for plumbing hardware. The Three Spigoteers seemed duly unimpressed. Next, he escorted them to the cheerleaders and jocks, who made a poorly disguised effort to be cordial; then to the Dramatiques, the theater club, whose efforts to be friendly were overdone— full of hammy affectations. Finally, Mr. Pennystacker led the Pretty Liddys to the Wunderkind Club.

By then, Fiona and the rest of the Pretty Liddys looked bored. Ebi examined the bright tips of her hair, while Heinrich intermittently broke into the Heinrich maneuver for no apparent reason.

Mr. Pennystacker wheezed to a halt before Roderick. "And this," he said, "is the Wunderkind Club, comprised of our humble school's brightest students."

"I'm Roderick Biggleton the Third," Roderick said. He stepped forward, extending his hand. "My mother is president and CEO of Beauty Goo Cosmetics. I'm sure you've heard of it."

"Who doesn't know Beauty Goo Cosmetics?" Ebi said. "Not only do they have the best lip gloss, they also have the best slogans."

"In Goo company!" Heinrich exclaimed.

"I loved your mother's Goo-for-Nothing campaign," Ebi said. "She's my makeup hero."

Millicent thought that "makeup" and "hero" were two words that should never occupy the same sentence.

Roderick's chest puffed. "That's my mother."

Fiona sidled up to Roderick, taking care not to get too close to him, then turned to Mr. Pennystacker. "You didn't tell me you had a cosmetics heir attending Winifred T. Langley," she said.

"We also have a fine musician," Mr. Pennystacker said.

"Yes, but even a decent-looking musician needs makeup," Fiona mumbled from between clenched teeth. "Everyone needs cosmetics."

Millicent had heard Fiona, but it appeared her friends hadn't.

Juanita stepped forward to be formally introduced to the Pretty Liddys. "I'm the musician," Juanita said. "Well, that's obvious, because I'm carrying a violin, although it could be someone else's, but then why would I be carrying someone else's violin? I mean . . . really. I'm babbling. Sorry." Juanita giggled nervously.

Millicent couldn't believe her ears.

"You should play the piano," Fiona said after a moment of studying Juanita.

"Do you think so?" Juanita asked. "I suppose you're right. My talent is bound to be easily transferable. Could you tell that just by looking at me? That's amazing."

"What are you talking about?" Fiona asked. She flapped her hand as if Juanita smelled bad. "I mean," she continued with a sour expression, "that violin is such a *tacky* accessory. If you're going to play an instrument, play one that's too big to carry around with you. Geez."

"I hadn't considered that," Juanita said. She looked dumbfounded.

Fiona turned to Mr. Pennystacker and said, "I thought you said these were the smart kids."

Tonisha stepped forward. "Hello, my name is Tonisha Fontaine. I'm a poet."

"A poet without a belt," Fiona said.

Tonisha recoiled. "See?" she whispered to Juanita. "I told you these jeans needed a belt."

"The tablecloth looks fabulous, though," Fiona said.

"Tablecloth?" Tonisha asked.

"That," Fiona answered, pointing at Tonisha's headwrap.

Tonisha grinned as if she'd been complimented.

Astonished, Millicent watched Tonisha. Tonisha wasn't the gullible type. Didn't she see that Fiona had insulted her—sort of? Fiona called her headwrap a tablecloth. Or was it a flattering remark? Fiona did say

Tonisha's headwrap looked fabulous. Millicent started to get confused.

"I wrote a haiku, a poem, about your shoes," Tonisha said to Fiona. "It goes like this:

*"Patent boots in blue*
*like the sky, they fill my eyes*
*no clouds block my sight."*

Fiona's face contorted. "What kind of poem is that? It's weird! It doesn't even rhyme!"

"I'll change it," Tonisha said.

Watching her friends being humiliated by Fiona made Millicent uncertain of everything she thought she knew. She shrank behind Leon, who'd been napping on his feet.

Fiona regained her composure. Her sights landed on Pollock. "And who is this?" she asked while staring him down.

"I'm Pollock Wong," Pollock said, avoiding her gaze.

"You look familiar," Fiona said. She circled him, apparently taking note of his clothes. "And dirty."

"Um, Fiona?" Paisley interjected.

"What?" Fiona snapped.

"You beat him in the art category at the Masonville

Youth Talent Extravaganza with your fashion illustrations," Paisley said.

"Zip it up, button it up, snap it up," Fiona said.

"Right," Paisley said.

Leon suddenly woke up and shouted, "Fifty-six!"

"Fifty-six what?" Fiona asked, alarmed.

"He does that," Roderick said. "He dreams about numbers. Leon is a math genius."

Leon extended his hand, but Fiona didn't take it. She seemed distracted by something on Leon's face.

"What are you looking at?" Leon asked.

"There's supposed to be skin showing in between those," she said.

Leon shrugged.

"Your eyebrows," Fiona said. She glared at Leon for a second, then screamed, "PLUCK!" She snapped her fingers at Ebi as if she were beckoning a dog.

Ebi scuttled toward Leon with a pair of tweezers she'd magically produced from somewhere on her person and started picking at the area between his eyebrows.

"Ow, ow, ow!" Leon shouted. He backed away, rubbing his forehead. Ebi put her tweezers away and shuffled back to her place among the Pretty Liddys. "Gee whiz, a simple 'hello' would do. What's your name?" Leon asked Fiona.

"I'm Fiona Dimmet."

Leon stared at her. "Fiona . . . Dimwit?"

"Fiona Dimmet!" Fiona growled.

"That's what I said—Dimwit," Leon said.

Fiona turned red. "It's Dimmet, dang it!" she shouted.

The Wunderkinder's eyes went round. Mr. Pennystacker snapped, "Miss Dimmet! Perhaps outbursts such as yours are allowed at your fashiony school, but that is not how we speak to each other at Winifred T. Langley. I will have to assign you a detention for this afternoon." He clasped his hands together under his belly and tucked his chin in, which created a whole new chin under his existing one.

"Mr. Pennystacker," Fiona said in a sweet voice, "what would you say if I told you I could take fifteen pounds and fifteen years off you without any exercise or surgery? All you need is Fiona's 'I'm Divine' Overhaul—or FIDO, for short—a makeover guaranteed to take you from dog to dream."

Mr. Pennystacker blinked at Fiona.

"I could make you look fantastic," she said. She waited a beat, then added, "Uh, because you have great bone structure."

Mr. Pennystacker blushed. "Do I?" he asked. "I did suspect I had good bones. So, I'd be very interested in what you have in mind for me. You know, I considered becoming a model when I was younger."

Millicent couldn't believe how Mr. Pennystacker had fallen for Fiona's flagrant change of subject or her insincere flattery. She stepped out from behind Leon. "Um, Mr. Pennystacker," she said, still clutching her backpack over her chest, "you're forgetting something."

"What? Me? I am?" he stuttered.

Millicent stepped a little farther into the open, but not so far that the Pretty Liddys could see her outfit. "That's right, you forgot something very important," she said, nodding toward Fiona. By reminding Mr. Pennystacker to discipline Fiona, Millicent would get even with her for being mean to her at the Mighty Masonville Mall. She felt a bit vindictive—a feeling she didn't like in herself, but she allowed it room to squirm in her stomach anyway.

But Mr. Pennystacker smiled. "How silly of me," he said. "You were supposed to give your speech this morning."

"That's right," Millicent said. "I have my speech. I even have my flip chart in the car. But that's not . . . I thought you were going to assign detention to—"

"Do you mind if we postpone your speech until tomorrow at one o'clock?" Mr. Pennystacker interrupted.

"Today is a rather special day."

"That's fine," Millicent lied. She stood there staring at Mr. Pennystacker. She felt as translucent as wax paper.

"Oh, yes. Fiona, may I introduce you to Millicent Madding." He gestured to Millicent and added, "Come, now."

Reluctantly, she stepped forward. She hoped that Fiona didn't recognize her from the Mighty Masonville Mall. In fact, she hoped that Fiona wouldn't pick on her at all. Mr. Pennystacker said, "Millicent's an inventor; clever and quick, this one."

Fiona smirked. "Not quick enough to get out of the way before ugly had a head-on collision with her outfit."

Heinrich guffawed, jerked as if he'd been electrically shocked, and nearly dropped his camera. Ebi shook with laugher, her straight hair almost making noise, like black matchsticks being shuffled. Paisley looked away.

"Oh, and the shoes!" Fiona exclaimed.

Millicent felt queasy, her feeling of translucence quickly replaced by one of conspicuousness.

"I didn't know they made shoes out of grocery bags," Fiona said. "Did you, Heinrich?"

"Are they recyclable?" Heinrich barked.

"What kind of socks today, ma'am? Paper or plastic?" Ebi asked, then giggled.

Blood rushed to Millicent's face in a prickly wave. She wanted to run or cry, or both. She looked to Mr. Pennystacker for help, but he looked confused. Then she turned to her two closest friends, expecting them to come to her defense, but Tonisha was busy reworking her poem and Juanita seemed to be searching for a place to hide her violin. So she stared at her feet, afraid to look up, yet pained to be facing her horrible, embarrassing shoes. What she needed was a friendly face, but if she lifted her head and saw nothing but jeers, she didn't know what she'd do. With the Pretty Liddy's laughter ringing in her ears, she chanced a glimpse upward. To her surprise, she did see a friendly face on the most unlikely body; a body in a gossamer blouse, green jeans, and high heels as pink as a bouquet of roses.

# *Four*

**W**hen Millicent got home from school, she slammed the front door and stormed past Uncle Phineas and Aunt Felicity, who were having tea in the living room. She bounded upstairs, not even stopping to remove her backpack.

"How was school?" Uncle Phineas called after her.

Millicent's footsteps thundered the length of the upstairs hallway. She stopped for a moment midway down the hall. She felt bad ignoring Uncle Phineas and Aunt Felicity. She could hear them talking downstairs.

"Now, what do you suppose that was about?" Felicity asked.

Millicent heard the clink of a teacup being set down and Uncle Phineas sigh. "She's at that complicated age," he said. "Yes? You remember it, don't you?"

"Would you like me to speak to her?" Aunt Felicity asked.

Millicent didn't want to talk to anyone, so she scurried into her room and closed the door. She dropped her backpack on the floor, went over to her closet, and flung its doors open so hard the knobs dented the walls on either side. Her cat, Madame Curie, who'd been asleep on the windowsill, bolted from her perch and ran into Millicent's bathroom.

Millicent glared at the contents of her closet, her hands on her hips. From left to right, hanging on wire hangers, were three skirts: one that was dark gray but used to be black, and two were year-old, denim styles. Next were three pairs of jeans and a pair of khaki pants with funny pockets placed in impractical locations. She only had a few tops, some of them flowery, tenty numbers that she'd gotten from a friend of Uncle Phineas's—Mrs. Gaia, who was a hippie. The other tops she had were an assortment of differently fitting, randomly colored pieces that had nothing in common with one another. The contents of her closet stared back at her like an audience. "I hate all of you," she said to her clothes. She started ripping them from their hangers and flinging them around her room. "I just hate all of you!" she shouted. Her eyes welled with tears as she threw more clothes across her bedroom.

After she emptied the closet, Millicent tore off her

shirt jacket and kicked off her shoes. She thought about the evil Fiona Dimmet—Fiona Dimmet and her horse hair and her fancy fabrics and her cruel little lips and her haiku boots. She plopped onto the floor, cross-legged. A tear dashed down her cheek to her jaw where it paused before diving onto her T-shirt.

A gentle knock on her door broke the silence. She didn't respond. The door opened and Uncle Phineas's head poked into her room. "Millicent? You didn't even say hello. . . ." He scanned her room, his eyes eventually landing on her. "This is quite a mess, yes? What are your clothes doing all over the place?"

Millicent burst into a sob.

Uncle Phineas's eyes grew wide. "Did I say something wrong?" he asked.

Millicent sobbed louder.

"It's okay. You don't have to clean it up. Not a problem, yes?"

Millicent sobbed even louder.

Uncle Phineas circled Millicent slowly and carefully, as if she were a frightened pet. "Your aunt asked if I needed a woman's touch in dealing with whatever's bothering you. Isn't that funny? I told her I had plenty of experience with parenting during her absence," he said. He picked up Millicent's new potato shoes and added,

"These are nice, yes?"

Millicent bawled.

Uncle Phineas's eyebrows arched. "What's the matter? What's going on?" he blubbered, but Millicent only cried harder. He wrung his hands for a moment before yelling, "Felicity!"

A moment later, Aunt Felicity entered Millicent's bedroom, took one look at the clothes hanging off the lamps and bedposts, and said, "This is either about weight or fashion. And it can't be about weight because you're a strand of a girl, so it must be about fashion."

Millicent nodded, her finger to her nose to stop the sniffling.

"It's about what you wore today," Aunt Felicity guessed.

"Yes," Millicent whimpered.

Uncle Phineas gasped. "How did you know that?" he asked Felicity.

"It's a girl thing," she answered.

"Oh, let me try," Uncle Phineas said. He studied Millicent as if he were doing a psychic reading of her. "Someone wore the same outfit as you today, yes?" He smiled as if he'd gotten it exactly right.

Millicent rolled her teary eyes.

Aunt Felicity chuckled, slipped her hand in the crook

of his arm, and said, "Really, Phineas, what a terrible waste of a guess. If someone else had worn the same outfit, why would Millicent have thrown her entire wardrobe around the room? And she's still wearing the outfit she wore to school. No, it's not one outfit that's the culprit; it's an overall style issue." She tapped her lower lip with her forefinger, thinking. "I surmise that someone made fun of what she was wearing. Am I right?"

Millicent sobbed in affirmation.

"See?" Felicity asked.

"Remarkable," Uncle Phineas muttered.

Aunt Felicity went around the room picking up clothes, draping them across her forearm, returning them to their places in the closet. When she finished, she turned to Millicent and asked, "Shall we discuss this?" Millicent nodded. Uncle Phineas sat down, rested his elbows on his knees, and propped his chin on his upturned palms. Felicity indicated that he should leave the room by jerking her head toward the door.

Phineas pouted but eventually rose. "I will leave you two to your lady talk," he said. With a sigh, he exited the room, shutting the door behind him as quietly as he could.

Aunt Felicity sat on the bed. With her left hand she patted the mattress while she beckoned her niece over with her right hand. "Come," she said. "Tell me what happened."

Millicent joined Aunt Felicity on the bed, slipping herself under the comforter like a secret note into an envelope. "It was awful," she began. "I've never been so humiliated. Even my friends laughed."

Aunt Felicity shifted and draped her legs over the footboard. She leaned back, resting her head on Millicent's shins so that she faced the ceiling. "It sounds terrible," she said. "Go on."

"There are some new kids at school. Heinrich Putzkammer is one. He's a photographer."

"Sounds harmless enough."

"Then there's Ebi Sato," Millicent said, the image of Ebi's hair still fresh in her mind. "But her real name is Leiko Sato."

"I was going to ask," Aunt Felicity said, "because I thought ebi was—"

"Shrimp sushi."

"Exactly."

"She's a makeup artist and model," Millicent said. "Then there's Paisley Slub. She's a fashion designer." She wriggled to her right so that she could lean on her elbow.

Millicent paused before describing the final Pretty Liddy. "The worst one of all," she finally said, "is Fiona

Dimmet. She's a fashion model." Millicent fiddled with a loose thread on her comforter. "She's gorgeous, of course." She wanted to add the word "evil," but she only thought it. The thought must have registered in her glare because Aunt Felicity nodded.

"Is *she* the one that made fun of you?" Aunt Felicity asked.

"Yes." Millicent sniffled. She went on to tell her aunt that she'd spent most of the day trying to avoid the Pretty Liddys—by and large a relatively easy feat because they had spent most of it in a special orientation class. She told her aunt that Mr. Pennystacker decided they needed to acclimate to a regular school.

"Acclimate? What kind of schools did these new students come from?" Aunt Felicity asked. She sat up and folded her arms. "And what are the chances of so many fashionable types showing up all at once?"

"They went to the same school, which is temporarily closed."

"And what school might that be?"

"None other than Pretty Liddy's Junior Fashion Academy."

Aunt Felicity nearly bolted from the bed. "That wicked woman has a school named after her?"

"You know Pretty Liddy?" Millicent asked, both

bewildered and impressed. "The beautiful, glamorous founder of the only fashion school for kids in the Masonville/Pinnimuk City area?"

"Hrrmph. Beautiful, glamorous . . ." Aunt Felicity grumbled. She walked a shallow arc around the room, her hands on her hips the whole time. She turned to face Millicent. "Electrolysis must've come a long way from good old-fashioned hair removal while I had amnesia."

"What do you mean?"

"When *I* knew Pretty Liddy, she wasn't pretty," Aunt Felicity said. "The Sprightly Sisters All-Woman Circus billed her as—" She came back to the bed, taking measures to make her every move as dramatic as possible. Crouching so that her face hovered scant inches from Millicent's, she raised an eyebrow and said, "Pretty Liddy—the Bearded Lady."

# Five

Aunt Felicity returned to the foot of the bed and sat, this time with her legs folded like a guru's, which gave Millicent a moment to catch her breath. To think that Pretty Liddy originally came from the circus world, where she earned a living from her facial hair, was too much for Millicent to handle. And to top it all off, her aunt had known Pretty Liddy.

"Looking at Pretty Liddy for the first time, you would have thought she was a man," Aunt Felicity began. "Even looking at her a second, or third time, you'd be hard-pressed to be sure of her gender. If she'd been wearing a skirt when I met her, that would have been a helpful clue."

Millicent liked stories—anyone's stories. She made herself comfortable, clutched her hands together behind her head, and stared at the ceiling.

"Anyhow, the evening she joined the circus, it rained.

We'd just done a curtain call on our closing night performance in Fair View City, many miles south of Masonville, in a farmer's field. After the performance, I wrote a letter to Phineas—we spent many weeks apart in those days—and I was closing the shades on my windows when a person wearing a trench coat approached my private caravan car. 'Sir,' I said through the window, 'the circus is packing up. In the morning, we're moving on to Clarity, fifty miles from here. You can catch the show there tomorrow if you like.' You can imagine my surprise when a feminine voice came out from behind that hill of hair."

"I'm sure I would have made the same mistake," Millicent said.

"Easily," Aunt Felicity said. "'Ma'am,' she corrected me, 'I'm a ma'am.' I choked back my shock and she said, 'My name is Liddy and I need a job.' She looked so forlorn, I told her to wait a moment while I put on my bathrobe, then I went out onto my porch to greet her properly. The wind shifted. Rain slanted under my awning and pelted me. Clutching my robe closed against it, I told her that new hires were not my responsibility, that I was merely the human cannonball. I told her I would take her directly to the Sprightly Sisters themselves who hired all acts. 'Acts?' she asked. 'I don't have an act. I'm a seamstress. I was hoping I could make costumes for the performers.'

"I nearly fell face-first off my front steps and into a mud puddle—a bearded lady, wanting a job at the circus, who didn't think she was an act?"

"That is pretty strange," Millicent said.

"Nonetheless, I grabbed an umbrella and brought her to the Sprightly Sisters caravan car," Aunt Felicity continued. "I don't think I've mentioned this before, but the Sprightly Sisters were neither sprightly nor sisters. Heidi and Consuelo were their names. But they both wore matching, curly red wigs to make them look as much alike as a Heidi and a Consuelo could.

"Heidi had come from Switzerland and was the child of trapeze artists, while Consuelo came from Mexico, where she gave guided tours of the ancient ruins at Chichén Itzá and was a part-time juggler. One day they both showed up for an auction in Pinnimuk City for a nearly defunct circus. They met and, instead of bidding against each other, decided to become business partners and bought the circus together. They argued for some time whether they should change its name to Heidi's Ja Ja Big Top, or Circo de Consuelo. Finally, they decided to pass themselves off as sisters, donning the red wigs—a compromise hair color between blond and black."

"Compromising is good," Millicent said. "But why weren't they sprightly?"

"Because they were perpetually cranky," Aunt Felicity said. "That wouldn't make for a very catchy circus name, would it? The Perpetually Cranky Sisters Circus?"

"I guess not," Millicent said.

"Back to that rainy day, before I lose my place," Aunt Felicity said. "I introduced the bedraggled Liddy to the Sprightly Sisters. They took one look at Liddy and, for one of the few moments ever, they were genuinely sprightly. *'Ja, ja,'* Heidi said, clapping her hands. *'Sí, sí,'* Consuelo said, clasping her hands to her chest. I could tell that they thought they'd hit the jackpot by finding a bearded lady. So, I told them to hold their horses—that Liddy said she didn't have an act, that she was by trade a costumer. You should have seen their expressions. They scrunched up their faces so tightly they looked like a pair of raisins. 'Hello? *Hallo?*' Heidi asked. She glared at Liddy. 'Do you not know you are having this?' She mimed tugging a beard on her own chin. Liddy looked down, but didn't answer. 'Hello? *Hola?*' Consuelo asked. 'You know you have this?' She pointed at Liddy's chin. 'Yes, I do know,' Liddy said after a few seconds. 'I've tried shaving it, but it grows so fast.' Heidi shouted, 'No shaving! You vill be Bearded Lady or no job for you.'"

"An ultimatum," Millicent said.

"Exactly," Aunt Felicity answered. "Liddy needed a job badly, so she joined the circus under the condition that she would be allowed to make costumes in her spare time. All went well for a while. Liddy got the stage name 'Pretty Liddy' from the Sprightly Sisters, who thought the irony humorous. Pretty Liddy spent most of her time doing her bearded lady act, which consisted of her sitting in a chair, armed with a brush and hairspray, styling her whiskers into animal-shaped topiaries, or 'topi-hairies' as the Sprightly Sisters billed them. When she wasn't doing that, she made the most beautiful costumes for the performers. She had such an eye for details. My human cannonball outfits were her creations."

"Like the one we found in the attic?" Millicent asked with a start.

"Indeed," Aunt Felicity said.

Reflexively, Millicent gripped the hem of her comforter. She wanted to see the costume again. She remembered most of it: the quilted satin of the cape; the shiny, embroidered leotard and its matching skirt; the tight-fitting, coordinated hood. There was a pair of boots that were quilted and featured wings at the ankles, like those the mythical Mercury had on his sandals. She'd only gotten a glimpse of the helmet, but it had left an impression on her with its purple and silver stripes. "I can't believe you have a real Pretty Liddy design," she muttered, unaware she'd spoken.

"If I didn't know any better, I'd think you actually cared about matters of style," Aunt Felicity said wryly.

Millicent blinked. "I don't," she said. Actually, she wasn't sure if she cared or not. Perhaps she did care after all. The only fact of which she was sure was that she still felt bad inside.

Aunt Felicity smiled. "Then you won't mind if I continue with my story."

"No, please, go on."

Aunt Felicity unfolded her legs and stretched out, draping her arm over the foot of the bed. "So, as I was saying, things went well, but after a while, Pretty Liddy began to behave strangely. She started with snide remarks aimed at the prettiest performers: Nona Phallophski, the trapeze artist; Anna Kannis, the dog trainer; and, in all modesty, yours truly." She flicked her hair back with her hand and guffawed.

Millicent thought her aunt's gesture wasn't at all modest. She wondered what it would be like to have a high opinion of her own appearance, to be so confident she could flick her hair and laugh at calling herself pretty. She couldn't picture doing it.

Aunt Felicity recovered from her outburst. "I can't completely fault Pretty Liddy," she said. "The Sprightly Sisters were partly to blame. Every time they'd see Nona, Anna, or me, they'd say, 'How beautiful, how talented, how charming. A star attraction!' And then they'd see Liddy and they'd say, 'Oh, it's the bearded one.'"

"That would drive anyone to be nasty, I guess," Millicent said.

"But Pretty Liddy's snide remarks were merely the beginning of her wickedness," Aunt Felicity said. "Things got more serious when she started tampering with the performer's props and costumes. Anna Kannis was the first victim of Pretty Liddy's evil pranks. One night, during a packed performance, Anna's dogs attacked her like she was a big hunk of honey-baked ham. We later found out that Pretty Liddy had lined her costume with slices of lunch meat just before she went onstage."

"No!"

"Yes," Aunt Felicity said. "Poor Anna was nearly nipped to bits by Chihuahuas and terriers and cock-apoos. She ran out of the center ring, screaming, dogs hanging off her A-line dress like ornaments on a Christmas tree."

"How awful."

"Imagine how Anna felt," Aunt Felicity said. "Then there was the disaster with Nona Phallophski."

"I don't know if I want to hear about it," Millicent said.

"It's not what you might think, though it is unpleasant," Aunt Felicity said. "Nona always began her act seated on her trapeze, which hovered near ground level. From there, she was slowly hoisted upward, to dramatic music, until she was high above the audience. The whole intro took some time—long enough for the glue to dry."

"Glue?"

"Nona's costume had a bustle sewn to the back of it," Aunt Felicity said. "A tuft of fabric perfect for hiding a small balloon filled with quick-drying glue. When Anna sat down on the trapeze, the balloon burst, spreading adhesive all over her bottom and the trapeze bar. When she tried to launch herself from the trapeze, she looked as though she'd go flying, but she just flopped over like a halibut. Stuck. She got booed because the audience thought it was all part of a lousy act," Aunt Felicity said. "There's nothing a performer hates more than being booed."

"Except being glued to a prop," Millicent said.

Aunt Felicity chuckled. "Except that."

"So what about you?" Millicent asked. "What did Pretty Liddy do to you?"

Aunt Felicity scooted off the bed, her feet landing on the floor with a soft thud. "That," she said, "is a story full of speculation for another time. Now, I must prepare dinner."

"But . . ." Millicent said.

"Yes?" Aunt Felicity said.

Millicent studied her for a second. She had hoped for some advice from her aunt like she often got from Uncle Phineas. But then she realized that her aunt's stories were different from her uncle's stories for a reason— they were, after all, very different people. "That was an amazing story," she finally said. "I can't wait to hear what happens next."

Aunt Felicity nodded, then moved toward Millicent's bedroom door without so much as a hint of the rest of the story.

Millicent watched Aunt Felicity leave. She had to give her aunt some credit—she told a decent story. It had funny parts, tense parts, and mysterious parts. It seemed as if it should have been complete. However, it lacked something. Millicent couldn't quite place the missing ingredient, but she didn't feel as warm inside as when Uncle Phineas told her a tale.

# Six

Millicent decided to go down to the lab, to look for Uncle Phineas. She knew she could tell him about how mean Fiona Dimmet was. She knew he'd have the perfect response. And she knew she could expect to hear a special word or phrase that would make her feel as if there'd never been a Fiona Dimmet.

When she got to the lab, she found Uncle Phineas standing at a table, at work on a new invention.

"Hi, Uncle Phineas," she said upon entering the lab. "What are you doing?"

"Millicent," he said, removing his goggles, "I'm glad you're feeling better." He smiled at her. Even his eyes smiled, which was made more amusing because his goggles had left red rings around them. "I'm developing a holographic bellhop."

Millicent sidled up to the table where he was working and peeked around his shoulder. There, on top of the table, sat a circular, wheeled platform the size of an extra-large pizza with a series of lenses positioned at various points within its base. At its center, a T-shaped, metal armature made of pipes reached outward as if it had arms. It didn't look like a bellhop, but she knew that the wonder of holographs lay in the illusions they created when turned on. She had a small holograph of her own in her bedroom, which appeared to be nothing more than a black dais, until she flicked a hidden switch. Then, it became a trick of light and form, modeled after Mount Rushmore, only the presidents' heads sang "She's a Grand Old Flag" in four-part harmony. She wondered what Uncle Phineas's holograph did when it was turned on. She resisted reaching for the remote control sitting near the edge of the table. Instead, she asked, "A holographic bellhop? You don't like the real ones?"

"I like the real ones just fine—if I can find them." Uncle Phineas said. "Many's the time I've waited, curbside at a hotel, for someone to carry my bags, my arms growing long from the weight of my luggage." He studied her for a second. "Would you like to see how it works? Yes?"

"Would I? Of course," she said.

"As I thought," he said. He lifted the apparatus from the table, then set it down on the floor. He fiddled with the remote control. Nothing happened for a second, then the base lit up. In a flickering of multicolored lights, the armature turned into a man, approximately Millicent's height, complete with a silvery gray uniform that had satin-striped pants.

"How do you do?" the man asked. "May I take your bag?" Though his lips moved, his voice came from beneath the platform where Phineas must have placed a pair of speakers.

Millicent stared at his face, which looked as real as any she'd seen on a human head. His outfit seemed to be made of wool fabric so supple it reflected light at the folds and creases. Even his brass buttons glittered.

"He asked you a question," Uncle Phineas chimed in.

"Oh," Millicent exclaimed. "Yes, you may."

Uncle Phineas handed her a duffel bag he had nearby. She took it and hung it on the pipe that served as the bellhop's arm.

"Right this way," the bellhop said. His wheeled base spun around, taking him with it. The tires lost traction, then they caught the floor and the whole contraption sped right into the lab table, causing a loud thud.

"Dear me," Uncle Phineas said. "He doesn't have the best sense of direction yet." He brushed off the bell-hop, making sure his face hadn't been damaged on the table edge. He smiled at Millicent. "Perhaps that's something you could fix, yes?"

Millicent wanted desperately to fiddle with the holographic bellhop. She was overjoyed that Uncle Phineas had enough faith in her to fix it. She smiled back.

"Mmm," Uncle Phineas purred. "Nice to see a smile on that mug. People say that a smile is a frown turned upside down. I say a smile is your teeth trying to get out of your mouth."

Millicent laughed.

Uncle Phineas stroked his beard. "Now, about your talk with Aunt Felicity. It went well? Yes?"

Millicent shrugged. She became instantly melancholy remembering the reason for her aunt's visit. "She told me about the circus," she said.

"And that helped you with your problem?"

Millicent didn't want to be rude by saying no, but she didn't want to lie either, so she avoided the question by asking her own. "May I tell you about it?"

"Me?" Uncle Phineas asked, surprised. "I thought your problem was about fashion. You heard what a bad guesser I am when it comes to that."

"It's about more than fashion, I think," Millicent said.

Uncle Phineas rubbed his palms together. "I'm all ears," he said. He sat at a lab stool and motioned for Millicent to sit as well.

Millicent made herself comfortable and proceeded to tell him about Pretty Liddy's Junior Fashion Academy closing and how some of its fashionable student body now attended Winifred T. Langley Middle School.

"I suppose that would put pressure on anyone to be a snappy dresser," Uncle Phineas interjected.

"The worst one is Fiona Dimmet," Millicent said. "She's pretty, extremely stylish, and terribly mean." She went on to tell him about Fiona's insults about her outfit and her shoes. "My own friends laughed at her jokes." Even in recounting the event, her eyes glossed over with tears.

Uncle Phineas retrieved a hanky from his lab coat pocket. "Just in case they fall," he said, handing it to her.

She took the hanky, mumbled "thank you," and dabbed the corners of her eyes with it.

"I'm sure this will come as a minuscule consolation, and I'm sure it will go in one ear and out the other, but they're only clothes. Yes?" Uncle Phineas said.

"No, Uncle Phineas," Millicent whined. "You don't understand."

"I do."

"No, you don't."

Uncle Phineas pointed to Millicent's heart and tapped the air in front of it. "I do understand," he said. "I understand that I could dress you in the latest styles or in last year's trends and neither would matter. I understand that whether you were admired for what you wear or reviled, there is an utterly unique heart beating in your chest." He took Millicent's hand in his. "It's like Halloween, isn't it?"

"Halloween?" Millicent asked. Millicent thought her uncle had unquestionably lost his mind. What was he thinking? Halloween was when kids *disguised* themselves. What did that have to do with being stylish? She frowned at him. "Halloween?" she asked again, more incredulously.

"Remember five or so years ago when we were low on cash?" he asked.

*Just like this year,* Millicent thought. She nodded.

"All we had to make a Halloween costume for you were old computer parts, some paper, and some poster paints, so we made you into an ink-jet printer from the neck up?"

Millicent remembered. "Mm-hmm," she muttered. "And from the neck down, I was a desk made from a cardboard box."

She'd wanted to be a princess. She planned out exactly what she wanted to wear, down to the tiara and elbow-length gloves. She even planned how she'd say "trick or treat"—with a British accent as soft and yawny as a

Saturday morning. Instead of granting her wish, Uncle Phineas had announced that, due to a sharp downturn in his invention's sales, she'd have to use what they had on hand to make a costume. Gone were her princess fantasies and her fancy accent.

"The best bit was how well you enunciated 'trick or treat' with a sheet of paper between your teeth," he said.

"Oh, yeah," Millicent said, though the memory of her ability to talk with paper in her mouth was lost among the larger memories of feeling humiliated that Halloween.

"The next year was a banner year," Uncle Phineas stated. "Diffollicle Speed Gel started selling like gangbusters and I could afford the princess costume you'd always wanted."

Millicent perked up at *that* memory. She'd gotten to be a princess after all, which turned out to have been worth the wait. Uncle Phineas bought a professionally made costume, complete with a red velvet cape. Millicent remembered she'd felt regal and special.

"And the beauty of it all?" Uncle Phineas asked.

"That I finally got to be a princess?"

"No."

"That I got to feel regal and special?"

"No," Uncle Phineas said. "The beauty of it all resides

in the fact that you always *were* a princess and that you always *were* regal and special."

"I was an ink-jet printer the year before," Millicent said.

"That's not what I mean," Uncle Phineas said. He scooted closer to her and looked her square in the eyes. "The costumes may have changed, but the essence of who you are has not. Whether you had a printer on your head or a tiara, you were special. Yes?"

"But I didn't *feel* special until I had a princess costume on," she said. "You don't understand." She'd come to Uncle Phineas because she thought that he would make her feel better. He'd always been so good at easing her pain, but today he was full of pitiful metaphors and awful examples. Today, he seemed to Millicent to be useless. She decided to repeat herself, though she knew it would do no good.

"You don't understand."

Uncle Phineas studied her long and hard, taking in every curve of her face, every freckle, every out-of-place hair. He touched the tips of her fingers, one by one, with his forefinger, as if he were counting them for the very first time. "No, dear niece," he said, with immeasurable patience in his voice, "you don't yet understand."

# Seven

**B**y the next morning, most of her conversation with Uncle Phineas had slipped Millicent's mind. She stared at the contents of her closet. Before her hung the most dreadful wardrobe ever in the history of clothing. Of course, she couldn't be absolutely sure of what made up the most dreadful wardrobe in the history of clothing, but she guessed that the elements of it were in her closet.

She sighed a sigh so deep it seemed to come from the first floor of the house.

She fantasized that she had invented a computerized fabric, immediately after seeing the shiny fabric that dressed the stage at the mall fashion show, and somehow made it into clothing. The fabric would allow her to blend in with her surroundings. She would call it Compmeleon Tex; part computer, part chameleon, part textile. She pictured herself walking down the locker-lined hallway at Winifred T. Langley Middle School, her passing imperceptible against the metal locker doors. She imagined giving her presidential candidacy speech in the auditorium, her clothing melding with the faded, burgundy velvet curtains. She'd be a floating head running for the highest student government office. Which might seem strange, but at least Fiona Dimmet wouldn't be able to see her clothes.

*Perhaps,* she thought, *I could invent a chic ensemble— something so beautiful and unique that even Fiona Dimmet would get her hem in a twist over it.* She didn't know how to design, but she wondered how hard it could be. Fashion design couldn't be too different from inventing, since both disciplines require making something from nothing more than an idea. Still, when she tried to imagine a stylish outfit, her mind drew a blank.

If she couldn't invent something chic, perhaps she could at least invent something that gave the *impression* she was fashionable. But, in order to cast that illusion, she'd have to know what was current to begin with and the only ones who knew the very latest trends were the Pretty Liddys.

Millicent threw her arms down at her sides. "Oh, what's the use?" she asked. No closer to choosing an outfit than when she started, she scooped up Madame Curie and set her in front of the closet. She knew if she dilly-dallied any longer, she'd be late for school. Drastic measures were called for. "You pick what I should wear to school today," she said to the cat. "You can do as good a job as I can." Madame Curie wandered into the closet, her tail brushing against the hem of a long denim skirt. Then the cat saw a ribbon hanging from a peasant top and started batting at it. Millicent removed both the skirt and blouse and said, "Thanks, M.C. Now I need shoes." The cat sat down on a pair of worn, leather-soled, slip-on shoes. "Done," she said.

Millicent got dressed with a sigh. What would her classmates think—especially the Pretty Liddys—if they knew she'd let a cat pick out her clothes? The whole scenario seemed to be a forerunner of a bad day.

Millicent parked her car and made her way through the school parking lot, past the Winifred T. Langley Memorial Fountain, and through the double front doors. She thought she might make it to first period without running into any of the Pretty Liddys. But then she caught sight of Fiona, Heinrich, and Ebi staring at their reflections in the hallway trophy case and primping.

Millicent ducked behind a garbage can without taking

her eyes off the Pretty Liddys. Heinrich was wearing an all-black ensemble, again, only this time with bright red sneakers. Ebi had on a fake snakeskin jacket, jeans, and reptilian-looking boots. Fiona wore a cloudlike, poofy sweater with a fancy, sparkling skirt. From the far end of the hallway, Paisley Slub fluttered quickly toward them in a dress made of layers of filmy fabric. The other Pretty Liddys stood off in the distance talking to one another, looking just as fashionable.

"Can't you hurry?" Paisley asked the other Pretty Liddys, "I don't want to be late to class."

Fiona glared at her. "Oh, please," she said. "Like I'm even going to need math when I'm a famous model."

"You're already a famous model," Heinrich reminded her.

"I mean even more famous than I am now," Fiona said. She arched an eyebrow as if considering what she'd just said. "Wait. More famous than I already am? Like that could happen."

Ebi laughed while Paisley said, "My first class isn't math."

Fiona glared at Paisley.

"I don't mean to correct you, but you said our first class is math? I'm not in your math class. Remember orientation yesterday? See?" Paisley said. She showed Fiona her schedule. "My schedule is different? But our classes are right next door to each other and we have the same second period—English."

*Oh, I hope they don't have Mr. Templeton for English,* Millicent thought.

Fiona clutched her eyeliner pencil in her hand so hard it snapped in two. "Don't you ever, ever correct me, you got it?"

"Right," Paisley said meekly.

Millicent watched the scene from behind the garbage can, feeling almost sorry for Paisley Slub. If she didn't know any better, she'd guess that Paisley got picked on by Fiona as frequently as she would have if she weren't a Pretty Liddy. *Poor Paisley*, Millicent thought, *she may as well be a Wunderkind.* She studied Paisley's outfit carefully. *On second thought, maybe not.*

The warning bell rang, signaling that first period was to start in five minutes.

"Wait," Fiona nearly shouted. "Look at this." She pointed to a flyer taped to the wall.

The Pretty Liddys gathered around her. "What does it say?" Heinrich asked. "Read it."

Millicent strained to see the flyer, but the Pretty Liddys blocked her sight line.

"'Announce your candidacy today,'" Fiona read.

"Candidacy?" Paisley asked.

Fiona snapped her head in Paisley's direction and glared. "If I need an echo, I'll go into the girls' restroom and scream," she said. She turned back to the flyer and continued reading, "'for class officers of Winifred T. Langley Middle School.'" She twisted her apple-red lips into a series of pensive pouts.

Ebi rolled her eyes until her pupils disappeared under her smoky green eyelids. "Oh, how ridiculous," she said.

"I think I'd be a great president," Fiona said.

"Ridiculously fabulous," Ebi said, suddenly animated.

"Read more," Heinrich said.

A lump formed in Millicent's throat. It felt as if she'd swallowed a Ping-Pong ball followed by a spoonful of peanut butter.

"'All candidates will give speeches today, Monday, after lunch. Speech times: one, sixth graders, one-thirty, seventh graders, two, eighth graders,'" Fiona read. After a moment she added, "Rats. That was yesterday."

"But, Fiona?" Paisley said. "Remember Mr. Penny-stacker said the speeches were postponed."

"That's right. He told the badly dressed girl she'd be giving her speech *today*," Fiona said.

Millicent felt a pang in her heart.

Fiona smirked and bobbed her head. "I think *I'll* be giving a speech at one."

"Why?" Paisley asked. "I mean, we're not permanent Langley students. It won't be long before we're back at Pretty Liddy's."

Fiona gritted her teeth. "I don't care," she growled. She paced a few feet back and forth like a panther. "If there's a contest, I'll compete. And I'll win. I always do."

Millicent tried to gulp, but her throat felt too dry.

"You should know by now how Fiona is when it comes to competitions," Ebi said to Paisley. "Remember the Junior Corn-Silo-Climbing Contest? She won, even though she's afraid of heights and despises corn."

"The winningest," Heinrich said.

"And what about the Guess-How-Many-Shrimp-Are-in-the-Trawler Challenge that was held down at the Fisherperson's Wharf?" Ebi asked.

"Won that, too," Heinrich said.

Fiona put her hands on her hips and glared at Paisley.

"What will your platform be?" Paisley asked in a hushed voice.

"Platform? Don't they give you something to stand on?" Fiona asked.

"I mean what is going to be your position? You know, what you stand for?" Paisley asked, then waited for a response from Fiona. When she didn't get more than a blank stare, she added, "How will you get people to vote for you?"

"Duh," Fiona grunted. "You ask the stupidest questions." She thrust her hands into the air with a flourish so broad she nearly knocked Paisley on the head. "I'll give them all makeovers," she said triumphantly.

The Pretty Liddys stared at her, not uttering a word.

"Well?" Fiona asked. "Tell me they don't need them."

Just then, three kids walked past and Fiona pointed at the trio. "But I'll begin with Mr. Pennystacker and some of the teachers," she said, "because once I win them over, the rest will be a cinch."

Heinrich and Ebi concurred, talking over each other about who needed what done and how urgently. Only Paisley was without comment.

Millicent listened for her name on the list of makeover victims, but she didn't hear it.

"What about a slogan?" Paisley asked. "My dad ran for mayor once? And he had a slogan. He didn't win, but his slogan was 'Vote for Biff Slub—a Mason for Masonville.'"

Fiona considered the question for a moment before saying, in a dramatic voice, "Vote for Fiona Dimmet— she'll make you look better than you do now."

"I love it," Ebi said.

"How much do you love it? Because I made it up on the spot," Fiona said.

"I love it lots," Ebi gushed. "You're smart."

"The smartifficest," Heinrich said, snapping a picture of Fiona. He paused as if he'd made a mistake, peered over his camera at her, and said, "The most smartiffic . . . the mostest smart . . . never mind." Then he snapped another picture of her.

"I'll be a fantastic president," Fiona said. She studied her reflection in the trophy case and fluffed her hair.

Fiona, Ebi, and Heinrich prattled away while Paisley looked on, dumbfounded.

Behind the garbage can, Millicent slumped against the wall, clutching the front of her blouse. She thought she might start hyperventilating any moment. Her feet slid farther and farther on the slippery, just-waxed hall floor, but she didn't notice until it was too late. Simultaneously, her feet made contact with the garbage can and it tipped over—*bam*—onto the linoleum tiles and she landed on her rear end.

The Pretty Liddys spun around to see Millicent sitting on the floor, surrounded by trash.

"Isn't that the weird, bad dresser from yesterday?" Fiona asked.

"Yeah," Heinrich said.

"In the garbage," Ebi said.

"Shopping for more dreadful clothes," Fiona said.

Heinrich and Ebi roared with laughter.

"Come on," Fiona said. "We have a campaign to start. I've got so many ideas. Like, I was thinking that every Tuesday the whole school will take the day off and go shopping. But *I'll* be the one to decide what everyone is supposed to buy! I think I'll start with Accessories Tuesday—everyone must buy a belt or a piece of jewelry."

Heinrich and Ebi squealed with delight.

"Or a hat," Ebi said.

"Or shoes," Heinrich said.

"No," Fiona said. "That's a different Tuesday."

"Oh, yeah," Heinrich said.

Paisley said, "But, Fiona? What if someone can't afford to go shopping? Or doesn't want to? Or doesn't even like shopping?" She glanced over her shoulder at Millicent, who was still sitting on the floor.

"Doesn't *what*?" Fiona asked. She shook her clenched fists. "Everyone likes shopping! I can't believe you're a Pretty Liddy. In fact, you're not a Pretty Liddy. Maybe you're an Ugly Langley." She laughed at her own joke, then abruptly turned sweet. "Wow. Did I just say that? I don't know what came over me. You're going to design me a whole new wardrobe for the campaign, aren't you?" Paisley nodded. Fiona gestured to Heinrich and Ebi. "Let's go," she barked.

The Pretty Liddys walked off, leaving Paisley behind. She looked at Millicent, then took off for her first class.

Millicent took a deep breath and realized her day was starting off as stinky as the pile of trash in which she found herself.

# Eight

Millicent counted herself lucky the Pretty Liddys didn't have the same first period class as her, but second period she had English and she remembered Paisley telling Fiona they had English then, too. Millicent walked to English class slowly and carefully, as if she were walking barefoot on sharp objects. When she got to the door, she paused. Straightening her outfit seemed pointless, but she did it anyway. A refrain of oohs and aahs came from inside the classroom. She peeked through the glass panel on the door.

Mr. Templeton stood in front of the chalkboard looking confused. Millicent couldn't see who was behind him, but someone was back there, pulling on the sides of his shirt, shaping it to his torso.

Millicent opened the door as gently as she could and slipped noiselessly into her seat as the final bell rang. Just as she set her backpack down on her desk, the person behind Mr. Templeton popped out. It was Fiona Dimmet.

Fiona cleared her throat. "So you see, everyone," she said to the class, "because Mr. Templeton is basically a long rectangle, with a bit of a belly in the middle, we want to emphasize his shoulders and deemphasize his stomach. His ill-fitting clothes don't flatter him at all." Mr. Templeton frowned and looked as if he were about to retort. Before he had a chance to say anything, Fiona continued, "And by emphasizing his shoulders, we would thereby draw attention to his . . . uh . . . perfect and very white teeth." She grinned at him. "Really, they're like little pieces of chalk."

Mr. Templeton turned red. "I did wear braces when I was younger," he said. "And I do use Doctor Glair's Whiter-Than-White Tooth-Whitening Coagulate."

"It shows," Fiona said knowingly. "But we're not finished yet. May I have my assistants up here, please?" Ebi and Paisley bounded to the front of the room and took their places at Fiona's side. Fiona whispered instructions to them, pointing to various spots on Mr. Templeton. Immediately, Ebi and Paisley went into action.

Ebi whipped out a tube of hair gel, a comb, and a blow-dryer from a tote bag while Paisley produced a needle and thread from one of her pockets. Ebi plugged in her blow-dryer, then started fussing with Mr. Templeton's hair, her arms a hair-styling blur. Meanwhile, Paisley went to work sewing up the sides of his shirt, then went on to altering the side seams of his pants. It seemed to Millicent like they'd been at it only for a couple of minutes before they threw up their hands in triumph.

"Ta-dah!" Ebi shouted.

Ebi and Paisley moved to either side of Mr. Templeton so that everyone could see him.

The entire class gasped.

"Wow, he does look slimmer," said a girl in the front row.

"You do notice his teeth more," said another girl.

"Yeah," said the boy sitting next to her. "And he even looks younger."

"Younger, too?" Mr. Templeton asked excitedly. "Does someone have a mirror?"

Ebi retrieved a mirror from her bag and presented it to Mr. Templeton. While he examined his reflection, Fiona stepped forward to address the class.

Fiona peered around the classroom, making eye contact with almost every student. Millicent ducked behind her backpack as Fiona's eyes reached her row. "What I've done for Mr. Templeton, I can do for you," Fiona said.

She locked gazes with the girl who sat in front of Millicent—Trudy—a pretty-enough girl, Millicent had always thought.

"What's your name, drab girl?" Fiona asked the girl.

"Trudy," the girl answered, paying no attention to the fact she'd just been insulted.

"Truuuuuudy," Fiona echoed, rolling the name around on her tongue. "We'll have to do something about *that*, too. It's a dumpy-sounding name. Anyway, Trudy, what would you say if I told you I can take you from frumpy to fantastic?"

Millicent thought that was beyond mean.

"I'd like to be fantastic," Trudy said.

"Starting with poor, bland Trudy, and with the help of my assistants," Fiona announced, indicating Ebi and Paisley, "I will give free makeovers to all who promise to vote for me for class president."

The class immediately went abuzz, the words "free," and "makeovers," and "class president" twanging in the air.

Millicent felt her stomach sink as if it were a rock tossed into a murky pond. She couldn't possibly compete with Fiona's makeover campaign. All she had were a few handmade buttons that read VOTE FOR MILLICENT and a stack of flyers she'd made on her computer. She thought about giving up then and there, when a small paper airplane landed on her desk. She unfolded it while the class went on chattering.

*Makeovers. That is so lame,* the note read. *I think you'd be a much better president.*

Millicent looked around to see where the airplane had come from. Paisley, who'd returned to her desk after helping Fiona make over Mr. Templeton, sat staring in Millicent's direction. She grinned and waved. Millicent turned around to see who Paisley was looking at, but everyone seemed preoccupied with Fiona. Millicent turned back around and Paisley was still smiling at her. She rubbed her eyes. *Impossible,* she thought. *Paisley Slub did not write this note.* She looked past Paisley. Next to her, on the verge of dozing off, was Leon Finklebaum. Millicent smiled timidly at him, just as his eyelids slid shut.

# Nine

The bell rang, sending Mr. Templeton's English class into action. Students filed out of the classroom, each kid wanting to be as close to Fiona and the Pretty Liddys as he or she could. They jockeyed for position, some of them pushing others aside.

Millicent looked around for Tonisha. She needed her best friend right now.

Suddenly Millicent got shoved from the right. "Hey, watch it," she grumbled.

Tonisha sidled up to her. "Sorry, Millicent," she said.

"*You* pushed me?" Millicent asked.

Tonisha stopped. She looked at Fiona, then at Millicent.

"Tonisha . . ."

"Girl, there's a makeover up there with Tonisha Fontaine written all over it and it's getting away." Once again, she glanced from Fiona to Millicent. "I'm sorry," she whispered. Then she popped her thumb and forefinger into her mouth and blew a shrill whistle. "Fiona," she called. "Yoo-hoo, Fiona!" And she was off like a shot, her headwrap weaving through the cluster of kids surrounding Fiona.

"Unbelievable," Millicent said under her breath.

She watched as Fiona, orbited by the Pretty Liddys, made her way down the hall, giving style tips to students as she went. How could she compete with gimmicks like makeovers? She shuffled toward her next class, her back slumped as if she were carrying a small person on her shoulders. And how could she possibly give her speech at 1:00? She couldn't. She would have to withdraw from the election. She slumped even lower.

The Pretty Liddys stopped at a corner. Millicent stopped, too, hoping they'd go in any direction other than that of her next class, history. She couldn't hear what they were saying, but after some discussion, Fiona, Ebi, and Heinrich continued down the hall while Paisley turned left in the direction of Mrs. Alpha's history classroom.

"Oh, brother," Millicent said. "Well, at least it's only Paisley." Then she thought about it more carefully. Paisley *was* still a Pretty Liddy—not a good thing, even if she did seem like the nicest of the bunch. Millicent didn't like hating anyone, but she had to admit her blood was now starting to simmer at the sight of any of them.

"How do I look?" a boy's voice asked.

"Roderick, I don't have eyes in the back of my head," Millicent snapped. "How am I supposed to know how you look?" She turned around to see him standing behind her.

"Wow," Roderick said. "That's an uncharacteristic outburst. What's wrong with you?"

Millicent knew from past experience that Roderick was not to be trusted with matters that involved feelings because he didn't understand them, so she simply said, "Nothing."

"If you say so," Roderick said. He lurched toward history class, talking as he went, expecting Millicent to follow him. She didn't like it when he did that, but she struggled to catch up to him nonetheless. "You didn't answer my question," he said. "How do I look?"

"You look like you usually do," Millicent said, panting. He always wore an oxford shirt, ironed within an inch of stiff, and khaki pants.

"What a relief. I thought I might have made a fashion misstep."

She thought about correcting him. She didn't say he looked fashionable—she just said he looked like he usually did. She decided not to say anything except, "Why would you be afraid of a fashion faux pas?" She knew why; she just wanted to hear him say it.

"Gee, Millicent. You sure are out of touch," he answered. "The Pretty Liddys."

They reached their classroom and Roderick slicked his hair back and straightened his tie before opening the door.

Mrs. Alpha clapped her hands to get the class's attention. "You're late," she said to Roderick and Millicent. "We are breaking up into historical sleuth teams."

Millicent grinned. She liked it when Mrs. Alpha gave out historical assignments that required research and teamwork.

"I've already assigned partners," Mrs. Alpha said, pointing to the chalkboard where she'd written down pairs of names before class started. "Millicent, Paisley will be your sleuth buddy." Millicent groaned almost silently. "And you, Roderick, will work with Angus."

"Unsavory," Roderick said under his breath. He took his seat and grimaced. Angus had the distasteful habit of picking his nose, which made him a less-than-desirable partner.

Millicent took her seat, too, trying to avoid eye contact with Paisley.

Mrs. Alpha cleared her throat with a gusty bark so

rough it caught everyone's attention. Once she was satisfied there wasn't a stray eye in the class, she went into a twenty-minute lecture on the glories of Masonville. She told the class that, in honor of the town's high historic standing, each team would study a famous Masonville landmark or site from a historical perspective and provide a multimedia report on its findings. Each team was to produce some sort of visual presentation as well as a spoken one. Artwork, photographs, videos, and computer graphics were all encouraged. From behind her desk, Mrs. Alpha whipped out a brown derby, turned upside down. "Teams," she said, "you will draw the name of your site from this hat."

From the Really Big Brick, displayed in front of Lulu Davinsky's Diamond Theater, down to the seaside and Fisherperson's Wharf, Masonville had lots of interesting sites. Millicent could at least look forward to getting an appealing location.

One by one, the teams drew slips of paper from the hat. After a few moments, Millicent concluded that all her favorite Masonville attractions were getting taken: city hall (location of the signing of the Masonville Declaration of Interdependence), Princess Dagmar's Castle (built by a woman who *thought* she was a princess but was really an heiress to a dental floss empire), and the Great Fence of Masonville (a white picket fence that ran from the ocean to, coincidentally, Princess Dagmar's Castle). Other locations were drawn, then Roderick went to the front of the class to choose for himself and Angus. He unfolded the slip of paper in his hand, and it looked as if he might be on the verge of clapping with glee. He said, "Madame Tournikette's House of Casts."

*Dang*, Millicent thought. *I wanted that one.* Madame Tournikette's had mementos of famous people's injuries, including the plaster cast worn by Lucca the Feeble Mason, who'd dropped the iconic Masonville Big Brick on his foot in 1887.

"What's left?" Millicent whispered to herself. She couldn't imagine anything interesting remained. Now not only did she have to write a report with a Pretty Liddy, she also had to write one about a minor landmark like the Masonville Zoo. "I swear, if we get the Masonville Zoo—"

"Well," Mrs. Alpha said, "as there's only one team left, I'll put an end to the suspense. Class, after I read this final location, I want you to get into your teams to discuss your strategy for your research and presentation. Your presentations will be due in two weeks." The class groaned. "Now, now," she responded, "that's more than enough time." She withdrew the lone piece of paper and unfolded it. "Looks like Paisley and Millicent have the Masonville Zoo."

Millicent let her forehead klunk onto her desk.

The Masonville Zoo had seven animals, including two yaks. The yaks were male and female, so they really had to be counted as one when analyzing the zoo for its variety of exhibits. With technically only six creatures, and a less-than-stellar insect display, the Masonville Zoo was passed over by most people for the Pinnimuk City Zoo that had hundreds of animals housed in natural-looking settings.

*Could this day get any worse?* Millicent wondered.

She felt a tap on her shoulder and turned around. There stood Paisley, as tall and as trendy as a boutique mannequin. "Hi? Remember me? I'm Paisley Slub? We're working together," she asked/said.

"Oh, that's right," Millicent replied. She didn't know what else to say to her.

Paisley pulled her desk closer to Millicent's and sat down with a flounce. "This project will be fun. I've never worked with an inventor before?"

"How did you know I'm an inventor?" Millicent asked warily.

"Mr. Pennystacker introduced you that way," Paisley said. "Yesterday?"

"Oh, yeah."

"Besides, I remember you for another reason?" Paisley

continued. "The Masonville Youth Talent Extravaganza? You caught the Mega-Stupenda Mart Bandits? I was in the audience that afternoon. Later on, I heard it was an invention of yours that stopped them."

"That's right," Millicent mumbled.

The bandits, three bullies who used to pick on the Wunderkinder, had stolen three bikes from the Mega-Stupenda Mart. They'd been hiding backstage at Lulu Davinsky's Diamond Theater during the youth talent show and Millicent had exposed them to the audience. Luckily for her, Juanita's father, a policeman, happened to be sitting in the front row. He promptly arrested the bullies and Millicent got written up in the *Masonville Gazette's* "Heavy-Hitting Heroes" column. Newspaper article aside, Paisley still knew far more about Millicent than she would have liked. She decided to stick to their history project and not get to know Paisley any better than she had to.

For several minutes they talked about the Masonville Zoo, but Paisley often attempted to steer the conversation toward Millicent and the Wunderkind Club. Every time she did that, Millicent tried to force the topic of the Masonville Zoo to the forefront. Finally, Millicent took a deep breath and was about to tell Paisley to mind her own business when the bell rang.

# Ten

At lunch, Millicent headed straight for the Wunderkinder's usual table in the cafeteria. Tonisha, Juanita, and Pollock were already seated with their lunch trays set before them, deep in conversation. She slid onto a bench and pulled her lunch bag and her campaign speech from her backpack.

"Hi, everybody," she said. They didn't respond. Instead, they continued to chatter among themselves. They were all talking about—what else?—the Pretty Liddys. Determined to change the subject, she waved her speech around. "Boy," she said, "am I nervous about giving this today." She was still pondering the idea of ending her campaign. She just needed someone to tell her she should push forward; that she'd be a great class president.

But Tonisha was on a roll. She couldn't stop talking about Fiona Dimmet's shoes. "Did you see them?" she asked no one in particular. "Were they not the most . . . Oh, my language escapes me. How would Heinrich say it? Fabulistic! That's what he'd say—fabulistic. Were they not the most fabulistic shoes you've ever seen?"

Millicent gasped. "Tonisha," she said, "you know very well that 'fabulistic' is not a real word."

"Give me one good reason why it shouldn't be a real word," Tonisha shot back.

"I don't see why it can't be a real word," Juanita said.

"'Fabulistic' is as real as any other word," Pollock said. "After all, who determines how real a word is? Isn't it by consensus that we all agree that a word is a word? New ones end up in the dictionary all the time."

"Yes," Tonisha said, "and I agree that 'fabulistic' is real."

Millicent felt as though she'd watched this scene, or one much like it, in a movie before. She tried hard to recall which film. Then she remembered. The movie was called *The Incursion of the Gray Matter Snatchers from Planet Zilthon*. In it, the heroine, played by Pinnimuk City's own Sigrid Herdman, found herself surrounded by friends who'd become zombielike for no apparent reason. Sigrid soon discovered that her friends' brains had been turned to mush by the Gray Matter Snatchers from planet Zilthon. Like leeches, the Gray Matter Snatchers took over Sigrid's friends' brains, thus inhabiting their bodies, so that they'd have new forms to take back to planet Zilthon. Sigrid assailed her former friends with a series of pleas to their humanity with no effect. All the zombies did was moan, "Uuuuugggghhhh, when next saucer to Zilthon?"

Millicent glared at her alien friends. She thought about reminding them about their love of the English language, but she suspected she'd have as much impact on them as Sigrid did on her zombie friends. Instead, she brought up the subject of the presidential race again.

"Boy," she said, "my speech is in one hour."

Tonisha was in the middle of telling Juanita once more about Fiona's shoes when she heard Millicent. "Oh!" she yelped. "That's right! I'm so sorry. Where is my head?"

Millicent gave Tonisha a smile, then said, "I thought none of you remembered." Internally, she chastised herself. Why had she thought her friends would desert her—especially Tonisha? Tonisha had, after all, stood by her through numerous disasters, mostly involving her failed inventions.

Tonisha gathered up her lunch and books. "I told Fiona I'd help her edit her speech," she said hurriedly. Without even a good-bye, she flew through the cafeteria.

Millicent watched her disappear. "Did I hear her

correctly?" Millicent asked in disbelief.

"Yeah," Pollock answered, "and I have some campaign posters to make." He grabbed his portfolio and dashed off, too.

Her friends were deserting her one by one. Almost afraid to, Millicent glanced at Juanita.

Juanita took a bite out of her apple and munched while staring back at Millicent. "What?" she finally asked.

Millicent raised an eyebrow. "Are you going, too?" she asked.

Juanita chewed—*crunch, snap, crunch*—for a few seconds before saying, "Nah, I can compose a campaign jingle anywhere."

Millicent gulped. Juanita had been commissioned to write a campaign jingle? The idea of having her friend write a catchy song for her hadn't even crossed Millicent's mind. She felt her stomach churn. Just then, Roderick and Leon showed up, each toting a bag lunch.

"Where is everyone?" Roderick asked.

"Helping Fiona with her campaign," Juanita whispered.

"Rats," Roderick blurted. "That's right. What kind of campaign manager am I?" He spun around and walked off.

"Is this really happening to me?" Millicent asked. She turned to Juanita.

"I guess I'd better go, too," Juanita said, her eyes downcast. She picked up her violin case and skulked away.

Leon set his things down on the table, slid onto the bench, and pushed his glasses up the bridge of his nose. "Let's see what my mom packed for me today," he said. He opened the bag carefully, as if it were made of tissue paper.

"Um, you're, uh, not helping Fiona run for class president?" Millicent asked.

Leon stopped examining his lunch. "Wow, Millicent," he said, "sometimes you're surprisingly not so bright."

"What?"

"First, I'm the one who persuaded you to run for president, remember?"

"Well, yeah."

"Second, do I look like someone who cares about getting a makeover?"

Millicent studied him for a moment. Leon had a point. He didn't seem to care whether or not his shirt and pants matched. Even under the scrutiny of Millicent's untrained eyes, his shirt and pants looked as if they didn't want to have anything to do with each other—as if they were having a silent argument. His hair had an unkempt quality, and, on occasion, he'd even been known to wear two different-colored socks as if he'd gotten dressed by hosiery lottery.

"But don't you worry that fashionable people, like the Pretty Liddys, will make fun of your . . . attire?" Millicent asked.

Leon peeled his banana. "I guess not," he said.

"Oh," was all Millicent could say.

"Don't worry. You'll be a fantastic president. And you won't need fancy clothes to be one," Leon said. "So, let's hear this speech. We've only got an hour to fine-tune it."

Leon's loyalty didn't make up for the way her other friends had deserted her, but Millicent was grateful for it just the same. She grinned at him. "Okay," she said.

# Eleven

The auditorium was filled with students, the walls pinging with the echoes of their conversations. Kids merged into clumps, then dispersed to various parts of the room to choose their seats.

Millicent listened to them all from the wings, her hands getting slippery with sweat. One by one, Mr. Pennystacker introduced the other sixth grade candidates for treasurer, secretary, and vice president, and they gave brief speeches. Millicent barely paid attention to what they said, she was so preoccupied with her own upcoming moment in the spotlight. She wished that Leon could have been there with her. Suddenly aware she'd crumpled her speech, she looked at the wad of paper in her grasp. She unfolded it and tried to smooth it as best she could, using her stomach as a flat surface.

In the dimly lit space across the stage, Millicent saw

the Pretty Liddys. Paisley and Ebi primped Fiona, while down on the auditorium floor Heinrich had already begun setting up his camera tripod.

Mr. Pennystacker swaggered toward the stage again and Millicent felt her throat go dry. Showtime had arrived.

For the first time, Millicent noticed something markedly different about Mr. Pennystacker: he had more hair than just the ring of wimpy strands that normally dangled off his shiny head. He had actual *hair*—a full head of it—brown, curly, and a tad recklessly arranged. If Millicent didn't know any better, he also looked thinner. He had on a dark suit (not one of the plaid shirts he usually wore with checked pants) and a magenta tie and periwinkle shirt.

He strode to the microphone. "Hey, everybody," he said. "Lookin' good, aren't I?" He tugged on his lapels.

Millicent gasped. Mr. Pennystacker didn't seem like the same cranky principal. He seemed more like the kind of large man who stuffed himself into a small sports car and drove around town showing off.

He stood at the microphone, simultaneously adjusting his tie with one hand and smoothing his fake hair with the other. Millicent squinted. It appeared that he (or someone else) had even trimmed the spider plant–like hair in his ears. "So, let's hear from your future class president, eh?" he asked the students.

Millicent wasn't prepared for such a bold introduction, but she came to her senses quickly and stepped out from the wing. A solitary cheer exploded from the audience. She looked to see who'd rooted for her. It was Leon Finklebaum.

Mr. Pennystacker turned to face Millicent. "Oh, Millicent," he grunted, "I forgot you were running."

Across the stage, Fiona stepped out from the shadows.

Mr. Pennystacker heard Fiona and spun around to face her. "Now, *this* is who I was talking about—Fiona Dimmet, who gave me a makeover this morning," he said. A round of applause came from the audience. He smiled broadly, then gestured for Millicent to leave, adding, "Millicent, you can speak after Fiona."

Millicent walked back to where she'd come from. Her head felt heavy with embarrassment, but she tried to hold it up nonetheless.

Heinrich stood directly below the stage, aiming his camera at Fiona. "Don't stand behind that thing," he said. "I can't see your spectaculosity."

Fiona came out from behind the podium and flung her arms upward, as if to say, *Tah-dah!*

Heinrich snapped a few pictures. "Give me attitude,"

he said. "Give me winningness, victoriousness, presidentiality—pretend you've just won the election!" He continued taking pictures while making his demands.

Fiona twisted herself into a succession of poses that garnered approval from the students, though they all looked mildly ridiculous to Millicent.

"That's right!" someone shouted.

"Work it!" yelled another.

Millicent peeked out to see who'd shouted, "Work it." Just as she suspected, it was Tonisha, who was up out of her seat, cheering.

Suddenly Fiona stopped writhing and yelled, "Touch up!"

Ebi rushed out from behind the velvet curtain with a fishing tackle box. She set it down on the stage, rifled through it, and produced a puffy brush and a compact. With a flourish, she dusted Fiona's face with powder, making the tiny jewels of sweat that had formed on her forehead from standing under the hot stage lights disappear.

Millicent mopped her own forehead with the sleeve of her shirt.

"Okay, enough!" Fiona yapped.

Ebi threw the brush and makeup back into her tackle box and darted between the curtains.

"Speech!" Fiona barked.

Millicent watched in disbelief as Tonisha ran toward the stage, waving a sheet of paper. Roderick rushed to the stage, too, and grabbed the speech from Tonisha. "I'm her campaign manager," he snarled.

"I wrote it," Tonisha shot back. Roderick offered the speech to Fiona. Fiona snatched it from him.

"Faster next time," Fiona said.

"Right," Tonisha and Roderick said.

Fiona went behind the podium and blew into the microphone. A dull whoosh filled the auditorium, along with feedback, which made everyone cringe.

"Welcome, fellow classmates," she began. "As you know, I am a new and fashionable addition to Winifred T. Langley Middle School. Many of you may have seen me in the Sunday paper's shopping insert entitled, 'Mighty Masonville Must-Haves,' in which I modeled for the Mighty Masonville Mall." She frowned at her speech, then looked at Tonisha. "Who talks like this? *In which* I modeled for—?"

Tonisha shrugged back. "Proper English," she mouthed.

Millicent saw Tonisha's answer, but she thought Tonisha seemed more apologetic than corrective.

"Whatever," Fiona grumbled. After finding her place,

she continued, "Or perhaps you've seen my picture in the ad for Doctor Pikkettes Dentistry Den. Maybe you've gone to Bagels and Locks—Masonville's only bakery and hair salon—because you saw a photograph of me on one of their shampoo bottles or on one of their doughnut boxes. I am a major marketing draw, you know."

"Oh, brother," Millicent said to herself. Did everyone really want to hear her catalog of accomplishments? When would Fiona wrap things up? Millicent checked her watch.

"I think you'll agree that my experience as one of Masonville's great beauties qualifies me to run for class president of Winifred T. Langley Middle School," Fiona said.

The crowd applauded.

"But in case you're still not convinced—" she continued. "Aside from my promise to give everyone who votes for me makeovers—"

Some kids who'd evidently heard about the makeovers beforehand called out, "You had my vote this morning!"

Fiona waved at them, then stated, "I propose that we change the election process."

"What?" Millicent asked out loud. She had a bad feeling about what Fiona was going to suggest.

Fiona placed her hands on her hips and pivoted to give the audience a three-quarter view of her. She inhaled as if she were dramatizing the moment. "I propose that we stage a series of three fashion walk-offs to decide who your next president will be," she said. A few kids in the audience let out whistles. "We'll have a runway built extending from this very stage," Fiona added. More kids whistled. "We'll have lights and backdrops and hot, hot music," Fiona said, her voice raised. The whistles turned into hooting and hollering, with some kids already giving standing ovations. "I am proposing three themed walk-offs; casual day wear, evening wear, fantasy wear. The winner of at least two of the categories, the most fashionable Pretty Liddy—I mean Winifred T. Langley—candidate will be named class president. So, vote for me and not that other girl with the bad clothes!" Fiona concluded, nearly shouting.

The students went berserk.

Mr. Pennystacker cheered and clapped his chubby hands red. "Oh, yeah," he said. "Fresh thinking. That's what I like!"

Millicent froze, horrified. Her bad outfit started to make her itchy all over. How could she possibly follow that?

Mr. Pennystacker grappled for the microphone. "Isn't

that a fantastic idea, kids? It's official. The next sixth grade presidential campaign meeting will be a fashion walk-off!" The crowd roared in approval.

Millicent shrunk into the shadows. She thought she'd make a great president because she was smart and hardworking and cared about Winifred T. Langley Middle School, but it turned out her classmates didn't want to hear that. They all wanted makeovers and a fashion show and a well-dressed class president. She couldn't give them those things.

Worse, she had no ammunition for tomorrow's fashion showdown.

She looked around the auditorium at the frenzied crowd. Then *The Incursion of the Gray Matter Snatchers from Planet Zilthon* came to her again. She tried to remember exactly what Sigrid Herdman had done in the final scene in which she discovered that the entire population of Pinnimuk City had been transformed into alien zombies. Millicent couldn't recall the details of what happened at the end of the movie, but she remembered the only thing that mattered: Sigrid Herdman had run away, escaping from Pinnimuk City in the nick of time.

# Twelve

Millicent pulled into her driveway with the din of the student assembly still ringing in her ears. She'd run out of the auditorium, not wanting to look back, not caring whether she missed the remaining afternoon of school, and not even caring if she got into trouble for cutting. Now her foremost thought was simply to get into the house. From there, she'd decide what to do.

Aunt Felicity was kneeling in the flower bed near the porch, pulling weeds. Tiptoeing up to the front door, Millicent paused to see whether Aunt Felicity had seen her. She had.

"You're home early," Aunt Felicity said. She stood, took off her muddy gloves, and walked over to Millicent. She placed her hands on Millicent's shoulders first, clasping them as if they were as fragile as porcelain eggs. "I hear that sometimes occurs," she added.

"What does?" Millicent asked.

"You coming home early," Aunt Felicity said, giving Millicent a hug.

"Rarely," Millicent answered. She hugged Aunt Felicity back lightly. Millicent took in the smell of freshly tilled soil on her. Uncle Phineas hadn't done much gardening over the years.

"It happens when you have a bad day, according to your uncle," Aunt Felicity said. "Not a good enough reason to run away, if you ask me. You're lucky you're smart, though. You can afford to miss a few hours of school."

"I'm not running away from anything," Millicent lied. She felt the sides of her face get warm. She hoped Aunt Felicity hadn't detected her red cheeks.

Aunt Felicity turned back around and put her trowel and clippers into her toolbox. "This *anything* you're not running away from wouldn't happen to be a Pretty Liddy, would it? What was her name, again? Fiona?" Millicent didn't answer. "Pretty Liddy herself almost made me run away from the circus." She turned toward Millicent. "And you thought people only ran away *to join* the circus."

Millicent sat down on a front porch step, suspecting she'd be there for a while.

Aunt Felicity joined her, asking, "You sensed a story coming, didn't you?"

Millicent nodded.

"You were right. But I'll make it short because I think you have a more important story to tell me," Aunt Felicity said. "I consider myself to be a strong-willed person," she continued.

Millicent couldn't argue that. Compared to easygoing Uncle Phineas, Aunt Felicity seemed downright feisty sometimes.

As if she'd read Millicent's mind, Aunt Felicity added, "I've even been called feisty—can you imagine?"

Millicent shook her head.

"But many years ago," Aunt Felicity said, "during a run the Sprightly Sisters All-Women Circus had in a town up north called Dairytown—known less for its butter than the fact that its residents taught their cows how to press the crosswalk buttons—Pretty Liddy had me over a barrel. Or, more precisely, *in* a barrel."

"In?" Millicent questioned.

"You may be aware that Dairytown is very close to Tumultuous Falls."

"Ooooohhh, yeah," Millicent moaned. "Seven hundred feet tall." She knew that a story that had a barrel and a waterfall and a woman named Pretty Liddy in it couldn't end happily.

"As I said the other day, Pretty Liddy was jealous of the performers she thought attractive. We'd been on the road for several weeks. In the course of that time she had targeted all the beautiful performers with her stunts and tricks. When the circus hit Dairytown, she had her sights on me. One day, during a dress rehearsal, I found myself, as usual, at the mouth of my cannon. I slid into the big gun, all the way to the bottom, where I felt something out of place."

"What?" Millicent asked excitedly.

"Pretty Liddy had put a barrel at the end of my cannon. I should have known something was amiss when she climbed in after me 'just to make sure' I was safely inside."

"How did she manage that?" Millicent asked.

"An airborne artillery artist's cannon is not as narrow as a regular one. I assume she hung there by hooking her feet at the opening. Anyway, once she was certain I was in the barrel, she placed a lid on it and, quicker than a carpenter, nailed it shut with me inside."

"How terrible," Millicent said.

"You're telling me," Aunt Felicity said. "Anyhow, I didn't know that Pretty Liddy had told the cast and crew to go on a lunch break prior to my entering the cannon. So, once I'd been nailed into the barrel, Pretty

Liddy rolled me all the way to Tumultuous Falls where she'd set up a booth with a sign that read 'Watch the Fabulous Flying Felicity Go Over Tumultuous Falls: $5.00 per person.' I didn't find that part out until later."

"Evil *and* enterprising," Millicent said.

"Yes," Aunt Felicity said. "Now, I don't know if you know this or not, but a human cannonball does not use a real cannon. Sure, there's a fuse, but that's for show. Inside the cannon is a springboard and the human cannonball stands on that. When the board is released, the human cannonball uses her well-developed leg muscles to help propel herself into the air. My legs came in handy that day. When I felt the barrel come to a stop, I kicked and kicked, as hard as I could until the bottom popped off."

"Good," Millicent said.

"I crawled out and saw Pretty Liddy. 'I knew it,' I said. In a rage, I kicked the barrel over the falls. Then when I saw the rickety booth she'd made, I pushed that over the falls, too."

"Good for you," Millicent said.

"Not really," Aunt Felicity said. "When I told Pretty Liddy that the Sprightly Sisters would hear of her deceit and treachery and that she would undoubtedly be fired from the circus, she glanced at the falls and said, 'Based on what proof?' She smiled the wickedest smile, then added, 'I came out here to bring you back to dress rehearsal, from which you so irresponsibly ran away.' My jaw dropped. 'You wouldn't,' I said."

"Unbelievable," Millicent said. She wondered how someone could behave so despicably.

"Once we were back at the circus, it dawned on me that I could still expose her. You see, in order for me to fall directly into the barrel, Pretty Liddy had to have removed the platform from inside my cannon. While I was examining the cannon, Pretty Liddy walked in on me with the Sprightly Sisters in tow. 'See?' she asked them. 'She wants so badly to leave the circus, she's tampering with her own equipment in the hopes that she can quit with an injury and get disability pay. How conniving.' The Sprightly Sisters looked at each other in horror."

"What did you do?" Millicent asked.

"Nothing. She had me cornered," Aunt Felicity said. "That night, I packed up my things in preparation for an escape. I had more than met my match in Pretty Liddy."

Millicent sighed. Aunt Felicity was surprisingly lousy when it came to telling feel-good stories. She wished the story had ended differently. Then she remembered that Aunt Felicity *hadn't* run away from the circus. She'd been shot out of her cannon and tore through the circus tent's top.

"But you stayed," Millicent said, the pitch in her voice getting high in her excitement. If Aunt Felicity couldn't be defeated by Pretty Liddy, then perhaps there was hope for her, too. She suddenly felt emboldened. "Pretty Liddy didn't beat you after all!"

"I suppose you're right. But it took plenty of self-determination for me to hold my own," Aunt Felicity answered. She regarded Millicent carefully. "How about you? Are you beaten?"

Millicent's noble heart shrunk back to its normal size. She allowed her gaze to wander to the top of the oak tree in their front yard. It seemed to her to be a good place to build a tree house. She imagined building it and wall-papering it with pictures of her parents and living there for the rest of her life. She'd survive on the food Uncle Phineas and Aunt Felicity would put in a bucket tied with a long length of rope. Millicent would hoist the bucket up every day and her feet would never have to touch the ground. And she'd never have to see Fiona Dimmet again.

"Millicent, did you hear me?"

"Uh," Millicent grunted. "Not really. Sort of. I don't know. Can you repeat the question?"

"Are you beaten?"

Millicent struggled to inhale gracefully. She didn't know how much to reveal to her aunt.

"Tell me about it," Aunt Felicity said.

Millicent decided to narrate her story in tiny chapters. She recounted the events of the day, from sliding into the garbage can to the ultimate humiliation of the student assembly. She managed not to cry when she got to the part where Fiona referred to her as "the other girl with the bad clothes."

Aunt Felicity nodded as Millicent spoke. When she was done, Aunt Felicity clasped her hands together on her lap.

"What are you going to do about it?" Aunt Felicity asked.

"Do about it? I can't do anything about it. I can't do a fashion walk-off. We—Uncle Phineas and you and I—don't have any money for the latest fashions."

"For goodness sake, Millicent, you're an inventor," Aunt Felicity said in a tone of voice both stern and empathetic. "Surely you've considered inventing something." With that, she stood and looked at her watch. "It's the time you'd normally come home from school. This conversation will be our little secret." She picked up her gardening tools and went into the house.

In fact, Millicent had considered inventing something.

She'd been wondering what kind of invention might help her out, but, like a hologram, it hadn't yet solidified in her mind.

After dinner, Millicent cleared the table. Aunt Felicity had made quiche, with the help of the Robotic Chef, a machine that Uncle Phineas had invented during Aunt Felicity's absence. Though it took verbal commands, could search through the refrigerator on its own, and could cook meals on the stove by means of long metal arms, it almost never got recipes right. Millicent thought that, if she had it a few more times, the quiche Lorraine with a pickle au gratin center could grow on her.

Uncle Phineas certainly seemed to have liked it. He leaned back in his chair, patting his stomach. "A special meal, yes?" he asked.

"For sure," Millicent said, taking his plate.

Aunt Felicity swooped into the dining room from the kitchen carrying dessert. Millicent was almost afraid to see what it was.

"Boston cream pie," Aunt Felicity announced. "Courtesy of the Robotic Chef."

"I smell old gym socks," Uncle Phineas said.

"Is that really cream in the middle?" Millicent asked.

Aunt Felicity sniffed around the edge of the cake.

"Smells like baked Brie," she answered. She set the cake down and cut a slice.

"Only a sliver for me," Uncle Phineas and Millicent said in unison.

Millicent sat down and took a sip of water. Ever since Aunt Felicity had challenged her to invent something to help her compete with Fiona, her brain had been on overdrive trying to figure out what she could invent that would give her the effect of being fashionable. She hadn't come up with any ideas yet. Just as she set her glass down, the doorbell rang.

"I'll get it," she said, still deep in thought.

She got to the door and asked, "Who is it?"

For a second, only silence answered her.

Then a shrill, unsure voice called out, "Hello? I'm from Winifred T. Langley Middle School? I'm not sure I have the right house. Is this where Millicent Madding lives?"

# *Thirteen*

**M**illicent stood behind the closed front door, her hand frozen to the knob. Her stomach felt queasy, as if she'd swallowed a mug full of olive oil. What was Paisley Slub doing at her house?

"Hello?" Paisley called. "My name is Paisley and I'm from Millicent's school? We're supposed to work on a project together?"

*That's right*, Millicent thought. *I forgot. Rats.* She opened the door a crack, but didn't let Paisley see her face. "Hi," she finally said. "It's me, Millicent."

"Hi. I can't see you? The door isn't open all the way?" Paisley said, trying to squeeze her head into the crack.

"Millicent," Uncle Phineas said. "Is that any way to treat a guest?"

Millicent nearly jumped.

"I guess not," she mumbled, then opened the door all the way. She invited Paisley in and introduced her to

Uncle Phineas. With the formalities out of the way, Uncle Phineas led the way to the dining room.

"You have a nice house. I like old houses. My parents like new ones? But I like old ones?" Paisley said. She shifted the large tote bag she had over her shoulder.

"Thanks," Millicent said gruffly, wondering what was inside the bag.

Uncle Phineas regarded Millicent curiously, then addressed Paisley. "That's very nice of you, yes? I like it, too." He looked down at Paisley's feet. "Oh, dear. Tsk, tsk, tsk," he clucked. "High heels are not healthy for growing feet. Do you not have a family podiatrist?"

Paisley stared at him blankly.

"A foot doctor," Millicent said.

"They have doctors just for feet?" Paisley asked.

"They certainly do, yes," Uncle Phineas said. "After you." He motioned for Paisley to enter the dining room and he followed her. Millicent watched Uncle Phineas glare at Paisley's feet.

Aunt Felicity rose to greet Paisley. "How nice to have company," she stated. "Especially such a well-dressed guest."

Millicent introduced Paisley to Aunt Felicity. She hoped her aunt wouldn't remember that Paisley was a Pretty Liddy. After Aunt Felicity's story, she thought it best to leave the name Pretty Liddy out of her vocabulary entirely.

"Please sit, everyone," Aunt Felicity said. "Paisley, would you like some Boston cream pie?"

"Boston Brie pie, to be exact," Uncle Phineas said.

"Brie pie? No, thanks. I don't like Brie. But I have a pen pal named Brie." Paisley said, edging into a chair. "And she spells her name B-R-I-E?"

"That's how Brie is spelled," Millicent mumbled.

Uncle Phineas smiled at Paisley. "Actually, it can be spelled B-R-E-E, too." Millicent pursed her lips. "I don't believe I've ever heard Millicent make mention of you," he said. "Are you new to Winifred T. Langley?"

Millicent glanced at Aunt Felicity, then blurted, "Paisley is here to work on our history project." She bolted out of her chair, beckoning Paisley to follow. "Come on, we can work in the lab. It's downstairs." After a couple of steps, she stood by the dining room doorway.

Paisley rose from her chair and said to Aunt Felicity and Uncle Phineas, "Thank you for offering me pie? It was nice to meet you." Then she chased after Millicent, who'd already disappeared into the kitchen.

She paused to catch her breath when she'd caught up with Millicent. "Do you always walk so fast?" she asked.

Ignoring the question, Millicent opened the basement door, flicked on the light, and descended.

Paisley trailed her as if she were entering a dungeon. "Wow, I've never been in a real science lab before. It reminds me of a dentist's office? Only I don't hear anyone moaning," she said.

"My uncle and I are *both* inventors," Millicent said as she went around the room turning on more lights.

Paisley scanned the room with an awed expression. "Your uncle, too? That's cool! If I could invent things? I'd invent a fabric with little lights in it or one that reflected light. That would be pretty."

Millicent thought that Paisley's fabric idea sounded like her own.

Paisley stopped near the Millennium Travel Cube. She studied the picture of Adair and Astrid Madding that was taped to the Travel Cube's door. "They're very nice looking," she said. "Who are they?"

"My parents," Millicent said. "They were inventors as well."

"Were?"

"They're gone. We're not sure where they are," Millicent said quietly.

Paisley stared harder at the picture. "They don't look like the type to run away from home. My cousin ran away one time? And she doesn't look like this. She looks more worried."

"They didn't run away," Millicent corrected. "It's a long story."

"Maybe you'll tell me sometime?" Paisley removed her tote bag from her shoulder and set it on the lab table.

"Maybe," Millicent said. She pulled up two lab stools. She offered Paisley one and sat on the other.

"What's that?" Paisley asked, pointing at the holographic bellhop.

"It's my uncle's invention. It's a holographic bellhop," Millicent answered.

"Wow. That sounds neat."

Millicent couldn't take the small talk anymore. "So, what are you doing here?" she asked sharply.

"We have a report on the history of the Masonville Zoo? For Mrs. Alpha's class?" Paisley answered.

"I mean, why are you *really* here? Are you spying on my campaign for Fiona? Well, don't worry. I'm going to drop out of the race. I can't compete with Fiona because the clothes you Pretty Liddys wear are too expensive for me to buy and I can't think of an invention to make me seem fashionable."

Paisley looked down at the glossy tabletop. "I came

here for that, too," she said softly.

Millicent couldn't believe it. Paisley *had* come to her house to get her to drop out of the race! She folded her arms so tightly her fingers tingled.

"You walked out before your speech today?" Paisley said.

"So?" Millicent asked.

"So, I think you would be a good president. I can tell you're smart? Because you're in that club with the other smart kids? And I can tell you'd work hard," Paisley said. She paused before continuing. "And Fiona is sort of mean. Not sort of—Fiona *is mean*."

Millicent was about to raise her voice at Paisley when what she'd said sank in. "You *want* me to run for president?"

"Yes."

"Did you pass me the note in English class?" Millicent asked. She stared at the Pretty Liddy, trying to process what she had just heard.

Paisley nodded. "But you can't tell anyone I'm on your side. Especially Fiona," she said, her voice low.

Millicent heard the seriousness in Paisley's last couple of statements. They didn't sound like questions at all but like absolutes. "I won't tell. I promise," Millicent said.

"I came here to help you," Paisley said. She unpacked

her tote bag, spreading the contents out on the table: a laptop computer, a big sketch pad, colored pencils, an assortment of rulers, and a bright yellow measuring tape. Finally, she pulled out a bunch of fabric swatches and fanned them out on top of each other like a dragon's scales. "If you're going to beat Fiona, you'll have to be fashionable. I mean, you're not a horrible dresser? But you could use a little help." Paisley absentmindedly fiddled with the fabric swatches. "It'll be like a trade. You'll help me get a good grade on the history project? And I'll help you become president."

"You'd do that for me?" Millicent asked.

"Sure."

Millicent flashed back to when she was six and wanted to be a princess for Halloween. Eyeing the sparkling, textured, colorful swatches of fabric, she felt as breathless as she would have if she'd sprinted five blocks without stopping. Asking Paisley to make a princess dress was out of the question, but it occurred to her that getting Paisley Slub to design her clothing was like her Halloween dream come true. *This is better than becoming a princess*, Millicent thought, *I'm becoming a fashionista. Not to mention class president.*

"But you'll only get a good grade," Millicent said. "It hardly seems fair."

"I really want a good grade at a regular school? Everyone thinks the only thing I know how to do is design. I can't stand it," Paisley said.

Millicent smiled. The arrangement still felt imbalanced, with Paisley doing most of the work, but at least Millicent had something of value to offer.

Paisley reached her hand out to Millicent. "So, deal?" she asked.

Millicent paused only for a second before she shook Paisley's hand. "Deal," she said.

With that, they spent the next three hours plotting.

# Fourteen

The next day at school, before classes started, Millicent sat on the lip of the Winifred T. Langley Memorial Fountain in a brand-new blouse, jeans, and kitten heels. She had to sit because, although the heels were only one-and-a-half inches high, she hadn't quite gotten used to walking in them yet. Nonetheless, she wobbled her feet from side to side to remind herself she had on high heels. Heels! To her right sat a duffel bag with her sneakers in it, just in case she had to get somewhere quickly.

During their meeting the night before, Paisley had sketched the top for Millicent. "I'll go home and make it," Paisley said, "and you can come pick it up. First thing tomorrow?" Paisley gave her address to Millicent, adding, "You can borrow some shoes. And wear jeans because they'll go with everything." Millicent showed up at Paisley's house extra early, but tried not to appear too anxious. Paisley answered the door with a grocery bag. "Here. You'd better hurry? Fiona's coming to pick me up? And she can't see you here." She handed Millicent the bag.

"Thank you so much," Millicent said as Paisley shut the door. *It's my princess day*, Millicent thought as she rushed to open the bag in the privacy of her car. When she saw its contents, she gasped. She put her hair into a bun and changed into her new blouse as quickly as a superhero would into a leotard. A bonus Millicent hadn't expected was the makeup kit at the bottom of the bag. There was also a sheet of paper with a face drawn on it, shaded in colored pencil—an illustration showing Millicent how to apply the makeup. She made herself over in a matter of minutes and drove off to school. Once in the parking lot, she examined her face in her rearview mirror before heading for the fountain. She didn't recognize herself. Though she'd never have used the word to describe herself prior, she whispered, "Pretty."

Now Millicent sat on the edge of the fountain, fingering the hem of her sleeve and occasionally sneaking a peek at her reflection in the water's surface. Paisley had made her a shimmery blouse, printed with an alpine meadow of flowers. Similar to the tops Paisley wore, it trembled in the slightest breeze. Millicent fidgeted her feet some more, inching them forward and back, enjoying the click of her borrowed shoes. Sneakers did not provide such a satisfying sound—they did not make your walk important. In sneakers, especially ratty ones, the world may as well not know you existed.

Tonisha approached the fountain, and her eyes bugged out. "Millicent? What is this?" she asked. She pointed at Millicent's top, then at her shoes.

"Hi, Tonisha," Millicent said. She stood, fighting to maintain her balance. "I *am* running for president, remember? And since the deciding factor is now a fashion walk-off, I need to contend, right?" She wanted desperately to do a runway turn, but she didn't trust herself not to fall, so she jutted her hips forward, then put her hands on them.

"Right," Tonisha said. After a second of analyzing Millicent's outfit, she added, "I've never seen you like this. You look really, really nice."

"Thanks," Millicent said. Then it suddenly occurred to her: as much as she despised the thought, maybe the way to get her friends back was to be fashionable. But then why should she even *have* to get her friends back? Shouldn't they have remained her friends no matter what? Shouldn't they now be able to see past her clothes to the real Millicent? She glanced away for a moment, wishing she didn't feel so conflicted.

Juanita and Pollock turned the corner of the school's main building and scuttled toward the fountain when they saw Tonisha. They slowed down when they saw Millicent.

"Millicent?" Juanita asked as she neared the fountain. "Is that you?"

"Of course it's me," Millicent said.

"You look . . . different," Pollock said.

"Let me get a closer look," Juanita said. "I can't believe it. You look . . . chic."

"Pretty," Pollock said.

Though she knew it shouldn't have mattered to her, being the subject of so many compliments made Millicent feel warm inside. She wanted more compliments, and more, and more. She wanted to collect them like stamps. She wondered if the Pretty Liddys felt that way, too—eager for the next flattery to help them feel great about themselves.

"Thanks, guys," Millicent said.

Roderick and Leon showed up. Millicent waited for them to notice her and they did.

"Hi, everybody," Roderick said. He studied Millicent for a second, then mumbled, "Gee, look at you."

"Hi, Millicent. I need to talk to you," Leon said.

Roderick turned to Leon. "Did you look at her?"

"Yes," Leon said.

"Carefully?" Roderick asked.

Leon studied Millicent as if he were searching for a flaw on her person. "What's wrong with her?" he asked.

"She looks nice," Roderick said.

Leon shrugged. "She always looks nice," he replied. Then to Millicent he added, "I need to talk to you." He gestured for her to step away from the group so that they could converse in private.

"You walked out on the presidential speeches yesterday," Leon said.

"I know. I'm not sure what came over me. I guess I got scared. But, you'll be happy to know, I'm staying in the race," Millicent said. She hoped her bright tone would erase the look of disappointment on Leon's face. "I'm stylish now. See?" She spread her arms wide, showing off her new top, and pointed a toe at him, displaying her borrowed shoes.

He sighed. "Well, we need to catch up on your campaign since you missed the speech."

"But none of that matters now. The president will be chosen by fashion walk-off," Millicent said.

"Millicent, a fashion walk-off? Have you lost it?" Leon asked. He paced around her, staring at her the whole time. "Even if you do win, you'll still have to be a good president. You'll still have to—"

"Look!" Tonisha shouted. "Fiona and the Pretty Liddys are here. Fiona said she would take me shopping with her."

"Me, too," Juanita said. "And she's going to 'do my colors.' I have no idea what that means, but it sounds special. Colors just for me."

Tonisha rushed toward the white car pulling up in front of the school. Juanita, Pollock, and Roderick loped after her.

Millicent watched her friends desert her yet again. She jerked her head in their direction, and grumbled to Leon, "And your point is?"

Even with her blossoming fashion image, Millicent couldn't compete with the free fashion advice Fiona could give her friends.

"My point is," Leon answered, "that you still have to be the very best you can be, despite the apparent lapse in good judgment the rest of the Wunderkinder are experiencing. If you do that, you'll remind them of what's important and they'll come back to you. I promise."

"I'd like to believe you're right, Leon," Millicent said. And she meant it. She wanted her friends to see her for who she was. "But once I'm president, everything can go back to the way it was," she added. "Besides, it won't hurt a bit if I win these fashion walk-offs either." She caught another glimpse of her reflection in the Winifred T. Langley Fountain.

Leon shook his head.

In history class, Mrs. Alpha had everyone get into their teams to plan how and when they would do their research and to divvy up responsibilities. Table legs screeched on the linoleum floor as the class rearranged their desks to get closer to one another.

"Hi, Millicent," Paisley whispered, while scooting her desk near Millicent's. "You look cool. Those colors are good for you."

"I can't thank you enough," Millicent said.

"Are you ready for your first fashion walk-off today after lunch?" Paisley asked.

"I'm kind of nervous," Millicent answered. "I'm getting used to the shoes, but shouldn't I train for the walking part? Isn't it hard?"

"No. Watch Fiona. She does it sometimes by accident? For example, when she's just walking down the hall? She puts one foot in front of the other. I mean, *really* in front of the other. Like she's walking on a tightrope?" Paisley said.

"Oh, okay. I'm pretty sure I can do that," Millicent said.

They got to work on their history assignment and planned to meet after school at the Masonville Zoo, to begin their project. Paisley offered to bring her laptop computer and her digital camera. Millicent said she'd bring her camera, too.

"I've invented software that has drawing abilities. You can scan in a photo of an elephant, for example, and tell it to draw, and it'll draw that elephant, or whatever else you ask it to," Millicent said. "Then it can make the image three dimensional. I call it Tri-Mension. We can use it to create our presentation."

Paisley couldn't contain her amazement. "Wow," she said, "I could learn a lot from you."

"I'll teach you how to use Tri-Mension. In fact, that'll be your responsibility: I'll send you the photos I take and you can use the Tri-Mension to turn my pictures and yours into three-D figures."

Paisley clapped her hands in enthusiasm.

Millicent had been wrong about Paisley. Her self-confidence needed work, but other than that, she was actually nice. She smiled and Paisley smiled back.

# Fifteen

The twelve o'clock bell rang. Millicent went to her locker, got her lunch, and went straight to the auditorium. She wanted to see how it was being set up for the fashion walk-off. She went in and saw two custodians putting the last section of runway into place. Another custodian stood on a ladder in the center of the room, installing a mirrored ball. A fourth custodian sat in a tangle of wires patching the stereo system. The speakers were as big as refrigerators and had been set up on either side of the stage.

"Gee whiz," Millicent said. Suddenly her breathing became shallow. Uncertainties taunted her. Did she need to be president? Why? Wouldn't she be happier with her nose in her books, minding her own business, doing her homework, and working on new inventions? Dropping out of the race suddenly seemed more like good sense than a cowardly act.

She felt someone breeze past her. "Don't be scared," the person whispered. "Remember—tightrope."

It was Paisley. She scampered to the stage, bounding up its steps just as Fiona appeared from between the curtains. Ebi clung to Fiona's side, dusting her chin with face powder. Heinrich followed with his camera.

"I can't trust you to do anything right," Fiona shouted at Paisley. "This skirt doesn't fit." She glanced at Millicent, who stood near the back of the auditorium. "Who is that?" she asked sharply.

Paisley shrugged as she looked at Millicent. "I don't know? I think it's that other girl who's running for president," she said.

"The badly dressed girl?" Fiona asked.

"I think so," Paisley said.

"Badly Dressed Girl, come here," Fiona commanded. She pointed at the stage near her feet as if she were commanding a dog.

Millicent made her way slowly toward Fiona. As she got closer, Fiona's expression changed from one of condescension to one of shock. A wave of crimson so deep Millicent saw it under Fiona's foundation swept across the Pretty Liddy's face.

"Who do you think you are, Badly Dressed Girl? Where did you get that outfit?" Fiona boomed.

"I, uh, d-d-don't remember," Millicent stammered.

Fiona's left eyebrow arched like a whip in midair. "That top almost looks like a designer original," she snarled. "And those shoes look familiar—like I've seen them on a fashionable person, not someone named Badly Dressed Girl."

"My name is Millicent—Millicent Madding," Millicent said. For the moment, all her fear of Fiona disappeared. "And I'm not so badly dressed anymore."

Ebi and Heinrich cringed while Paisley slapped her palms to her face.

"What?" Fiona barked. She went to the edge of the stage so that she looked down on Millicent. "Perhaps we should change your name, then, to You-Can-Dress-Me-Up-but-I'm-Still-a-Geek Girl."

The custodian who'd been patching the stereo wires stood. "Done," he said. "Ready for music."

Fiona suddenly went from dark to bright. "Oh," she said, "thank you so much for hooking up the stereo, Mr. Custodian." She turned to Ebi and growled, "Get the music in there."

Ebi scampered backstage, then returned a few seconds later with a CD in her hand. She ran to the stereo and inserted it. Immediately, the auditorium shivered with the thump-thump-chingy-chingy-thump of dance music.

Millicent felt it rattle her internal organs. She thought that even a person with terrible rhythm would be able to walk to a tune played that loudly.

Fiona started tapping her feet.

"Give us a preview," Heinrich shouted.

"Walk it out," Ebi shouted.

"Prance it like a pretty pony," Heinrich shouted.

"Oooooooohhhh," Fiona squealed. "I love to walk."

Paisley stood behind the other Pretty Liddys, gesturing in her own made-up sign language to Millicent. *Watch her,* she seemed to be saying.

"Oooooooohhhh," Fiona squealed again. "I can't help myself any longer. I have to walk NOW!" She threw her shoulders back, jutted her hips out, and pitched forward onto the runway.

Just as Paisley had said she would, Fiona walked by placing one foot, very definitely, in front of the other. Millicent stood watching her. She thought it wouldn't be a difficult walk to imitate because it reminded her of the way Lipizzaner stallions pranced. She had been a big fan of the horses when she was younger.

Again, Millicent glanced at Paisley, who seemed to be signing, *Watch her turn.* Millicent caught sight of Fiona just in time to see her arrive at the end of the runway, where she stopped, stared at the empty auditorium, then spun around and flounced back up the runway to the stage.

Fiona fanned herself with her hand. "Was it good?" she asked the Pretty Liddys.

"Oh, yes," Ebi said.

"Incrediblisitic," Heinrich said.

"Really? I thought so, too," Fiona said, flicking her hair back. "It just felt right, you know?"

Paisley was trying to tell Millicent something else. She hung her arms at her side as if they were marionettes' arms with their strings cut. "Oh," Millicent whispered. She understood that she was supposed to walk with her arms dangling.

"What's going on here?" Fiona asked sharply. She glared at Paisley and then at Millicent. "What are you two saying to each other?"

"Uh," Paisley grunted.

Just then, the earliest students wandered into the auditorium. They shuffled toward the first and second rows of seats.

"They can't see me before the walk-off," Fiona shouted, then ran between the curtains to the backstage area. The Pretty Liddys scampered after her.

Millicent went backstage, too. Standing by the wings, she clutched at her stomach, catching her thumbs on her borrowed belt. She couldn't tell whether the gripping sensation in her throat was nerves or dread because she was about to betray everything she stood for.

"Welcome, Langley students!" Mr. Pennystacker boomed into the microphone. Today, he wore a dark blue suit, a light green shirt, and an orange tie. His new hair was slicked back and tucked behind his ears. "What's up? Are you ready for the first fashion walk-off for class president?"

"Yeah!" several kids hollered.

"All walk-offs for sixth grade class president will have themes, which have been decided in advance by yours truly based on a list of possibilities provided by one of our new students, Ebi Sato," he stated. Ebi stepped out from the wings, did a fashion pose, then scampered backstage. "Each upcoming theme has been posted on the student activity board along with corresponding dates. As you've probably seen, today's theme is casual day wear, or 'Belt It and Go,'" Mr. Pennystacker continued. "Remember, the candidate who wins two of the three walk-offs will be your new president."

"All right!" a few kids yelled.

"All right!" Mr. Pennystacker yelled back. "We'll judge

this event by a round of applause at the end. Let's begin with your first candidate, Fiona Dimmet!" He raised his arm and the lights faded.

Almost immediately, pounding music filled the auditorium. Millicent tapped her toes. She remembered when she was little and Uncle Phineas had tried to teach her ballroom dancing on a Saturday afternoon when they had nothing to waste but time. "Millicent, dear," he'd said, "dancing is terrific because it's math and heart all rolled into an aerobic exercise, yes? Count to the music and, most importantly, *feel* it." Just remembering Uncle Phineas put her at relative ease. She closed her eyes and let the drumbeats rattle her rib cage until everything about her felt like rhythm.

Wild cheering startled Millicent from her trance. She peered out from behind the curtains to see Fiona pause at the end of the runway and stare out at the frenzied audience. They loved Fiona Dimmet—Fiona Dimmet and her hair-o-plenty, Fiona Dimmet and her teeth so white, Fiona Dimmet and her fashionable clothes. Suddenly Millicent's palms started to sweat. What if she couldn't do it? What if Fiona really became president?

Fiona went backstage to thunderous applause. "Top that, Dressed-Up-Normally-Badly-Dressed Girl," she said to Millicent. She tossed her hair back, then joined the Pretty Liddys, who congregated around her—all except Paisley, who gave Millicent the thumbs-up sign. "Good luck," Paisley mouthed.

The music went down and Millicent heard Mr. Pennystacker say, "And now, our second candidate, Millicent Madding." A wave of polite clapping coursed through the crowd. Then the music started up again.

Millicent looked back at the Pretty Liddys. Fiona folded her arms and gave a smile as thin and as phony as her pouty lips would allow. "Don't fall," Fiona said smugly.

A surge of heat gushed up Millicent's cheeks. At first she thought it was embarrassment, but it wasn't. It was anger. She decided she would show Fiona Dimmet a thing or two. She thrust her shoulders back and threw back the curtains. Her eyes landed on the front row of seats where the other Pretty Liddy students sat. They'd be the first to boo her if she made a mistake.

She closed her eyes. "Count to the music and feel it," she whispered to herself. *One, two, three, four,* she thought to the beat.

Something inside took hold, regulating her as if she were a radio-controlled hobby airplane, and she launched herself into motion, high-stepping to the raucous beat. She reached the runway with the same ease as she would have if she'd had on sneakers. In her heart she felt almost as pretty as Fiona Dimmet herself. She pooched out her lower lip as she'd seen Fiona do, and tried to look as bored as possible.

"Don't fall, geekette!" Ebi shouted from between the curtains. "Just kidding. Do!"

Millicent's high-heeled foot landed unsurely and her ankle buckled. She came to a halt, teetering like she'd been pushed, her arms flailing to keep her balance. The students gasped. *No,* she thought, *I'm going to be president.* She summoned her determination and regained her posture.

With a huff of fortitude, she resumed her walk down the runway, now with a renewed sense of spirit. She reached the end of the runway, planted her hands on her hips, and pouted at the crowd. Her eyes scanned the room and landed on a solitary face that seemed completely unimpressed—Leon Finklebaum's. Millicent stared at him a split second longer and realized she had been mistaken. He wasn't unimpressed—he was disgusted. *Well, too bad,* she thought. Then she turned to head back up the runway to the sound of cheering the likes of which she'd never heard before.

The buoyancy of the cheers would have been enough to carry her all the way back to her destination—the gap between the velvet curtains. But there, with the curtains gathered by her fists around her face, was Fiona, glowering at her. It occurred to Millicent that Fiona looked like one of the Australian frilled lizards she'd seen on a nature special on television. They had bone and skin collars that fanned out when they were aggravated. Cross them and they hissed at you and ran at you, mouths wide open, their collars fanned out in rage. Fiona snapped the curtains shut in Millicent's face.

"Wasn't that something, kids?" Mr. Pennystacker said, clapping. The audience whooped in response. "If I may have our two candidates onstage, please."

Both Fiona and Millicent took center stage, each trying not to look at the other. Fiona waved like a queen at the audience. Millicent caught the gesture out of the corner of her eye and waved, too.

"There's something very wrong going on here," Fiona hissed sidelong at Millicent. "And I'm going to find out what it is."

# Sixteen

Millicent waited at the front gate of the Masonville Zoo after school, her thoughts still fuzzy, happy, and a little bit confused. Mostly, she was tired. She leaned against the gate and let the cool metal rail dig into her back.

Paisley approached a moment later, half walking, half galloping in her high heels toward Millicent. "I can't believe it," she puffed, without any upward inflection, when she reached Millicent. She bent over to catch her breath. "I can't believe you tied with Fiona."

"Me neither," Millicent said. "It's all because of you that I look so nice. Thank you."

"It's no problem," Paisley said bashfully. "That's what I do. I make clothes."

"How is Fiona doing?"

"The maddest I've ever seen her," Paisley said. "She was, like, red? Well, more like a bright coral color? With magenta spots. Anyway, after Mr. Pennystacker announced the tie, she stormed off. You saw that, right?"

"How could I have missed it?" Still etched in Millicent's memory was the moment when Mr. Pennystacker had held his hand, first over Fiona's head, then Millicent's. He couldn't gauge the audience's response because both girls had gotten the same uproarious level of applause. With a shrug, he had announced the first presidential fashion walk-off a tie.

"Later? Ebi and Heinrich tried to make her feel better," Paisley continued, "but she kept staring at me? And staring at me? And she said, 'I smell a traitor,' but I didn't even blink." She laughed.

Millicent smiled at Paisley. After all that Paisley had done for her, the last thing she wanted was to get her into trouble with Fiona. She stuffed her worry down and tried to change the subject.

"Speaking of traitors, I wonder what my friends thought. Tonisha, Juanita, Pollock, and Roderick are on *her* campaign committee." Millicent wondered if they might now reconsider their affiliations. Maybe her friends would come back to her, begging for forgiveness. Despite her hurt feelings, she felt the pang of missing them. Maybe they had seen the error of their ways and were missing her, too.

Millicent shook off the fantasy. She gestured toward the zoo entrance. "Shall we?" she asked.

Millicent and Paisley spent the next two hours touring the grounds, taking notes, and grabbing as many brochures as they could get their hands on. Paisley took plenty of pictures, which she said she would later download into her computer. Millicent took notes with an invention of hers: the Dictation Microphone Pen, a cylinder the size of a paper towel tube, into which she spoke as one would a microphone. When she finished speaking, she'd run the ink tip of the pen along a sheet of paper and the pen would write what she'd just spoken. She invented it because sometimes thoughts came to her so quickly she didn't have time to write them down before they went away. She hadn't quite solved the problem of the device recording every sound it heard, so her notes came out with Paisley's exclamations of "Oh, that's so cool!" and "You're so smart!" sprinkled throughout.

As the two of them took photos and notes on the animals—the two yaks, a zebra, an elephant, a chimpanzee, and an otter—Millicent explained to Paisley how to take the best pictures for the Tri-Mension software: from many angles. "This is how I photograph my own designs, too," Paisley said. "I like to have a record of my work. I keep it on my computer."

After a while, Millicent noticed that Paisley seemed a bit scatterbrained. On occasion, she'd take a picture of an animal, only to forget she'd already taken one, or worse, forget where she'd put her camera, which she'd never removed from the strap that hung from her neck. Millicent would point to the camera and Paisley would grunt, "Duh?" Millicent knew she wasn't stupid, because designing certainly took a brand of smarts and creativity. Nonetheless, she did think Paisley could use a memory jogger like a little tape recorder to remind her of important things or at least a string tied around her finger.

They stopped at the last animal, the rhino.

Paisley stuck her fingers through the chain-link fence as if she wished her fingers were long enough to touch the rhinoceros. "I like this animal? Because it's wrinkled? Like a big, unrolled bolt of gray velvet," Paisley said. "Oh, did I lose my camera?"

"No," Millicent said and jerked her head to indicate it was still around Paisley's neck.

"Duh," Paisley murmured. She took a picture of the rhino.

Millicent took note of when the rhino had been acquired, monitoring Paisley the whole time. She decided she'd have to keep a close eye on her to make sure they kept everything organized for their history project.

With the large animals out of the way, they moved on to a building called Mr. Ento's Bugopolis, where the insect exhibits were housed. The outside of the building featured a stucco relief of a city, complete with sculptured ants crawling over its surface, which gave one the impression that Mr. Ento's Bugopolis would be especially fancy inside. Millicent knew otherwise. Nevertheless, she took one of the brochures that outlined when Mr. Ento's was erected.

"'Mr. Ento's Bugopolis was founded in 1945,'" Millicent read to Paisley. "'It was the first building of the Masonville Zoo and was erected purely as a roadside attraction. It was Masonville's only gas station and insect zoo.'" She paused. "I didn't even know that."

"See? We're both learning stuff. Cool, huh?" Paisley said.

They went inside. In the center of the room was an all-glass display case the size of a station wagon. Partitions divided the box into four sections, and a lid kept the whole thing intact. Each section had a small, crudely made plaster building, as if each had been created as a preschool craft project. Hundreds of bugs crawled in, around, and through each building.

"These are so pretty," Paisley said. "Look at the colors."

Once again, Millicent noticed that Paisley's voice didn't

go up at the ends of her sentences.

Paisley went over to the nearest section of the display, the corner where a mass of beetles scurried around in a greenish, purplish, blackish wave. She fumbled for her camera—much to Millicent's delight, Paisley knew where to find it—and took several pictures. She photographed a particular beetle as it skittered in a circle. She must have gotten the bug from every angle.

Millicent had to admit, she liked seeing the world through Paisley's eyes. To Paisley, everything was reduced to color or shape or texture, not knowledge to be remembered. It didn't matter to her that the scarab beetles' scientific name was Scarabaeidae, or that coleoptera was the name for beetles in general. She experienced the world just as it appeared, not as facts to be entered in a notebook or keyed into a computer. Millicent decided that perhaps that was the best trait she'd come across in a person in a very long time. Who cared if she forgot she had something as obvious as a camera hanging around her neck? Paisley's single shortcoming didn't matter to Millicent.

# Seventeen

On Monday morning, Millicent left for Paisley's house to retrieve her secret paper bag. She and Paisley had agreed that every other day, until the final presidential walk-off, Millicent would go to Paisley's house for a top, a pair of pants, skirt, or complete outfit. Paisley couldn't make an outfit every day and still keep up with her homework. But she felt confident she could maintain Millicent's status as a stylish candidate most of the time.

Millicent pulled up about half a block from Paisley's house. She gripped the steering wheel for a second, as excited as she was the first time Paisley left her an ensemble. She turned off the engine and walked the rest of the way, padding up the front walk to the porch as quietly as she could. Something rustled in the hedges that lined the path and she stopped in her tracks to listen. Satisfied it wasn't a big dog, she continued forward.

The bag sat on the porch, just like before, like a

brown paper treasure chest. She couldn't contain herself, so she peeked inside. A pair of pants lay neatly folded at the bottom of the bag. Millicent smiled. She shifted the pants and saw there was also a sweater and a pair of shoes. She crunched the sack closed and heard the rustling in the hedge once again.

Feeling slightly uneasy, she got up and scampered down the walk toward her car. Once safely inside, she breathed a sigh of relief and started the engine.

Driving past Paisley's house, she saw Fiona on the porch, her hands on her hips. She was glaring at Millicent. *Oh, no*, Millicent thought, *was that Fiona that I heard in the bushes?* She sped off, putting as much distance between herself and Fiona as she could.

Millicent got to school extra early, so she had time to go to the girls' room to change into her new clothes. The pants were made of a satiny, steel blue fabric and had pockets with flaps and shiny buttons. The sweater was pistachio green and softer than any sweater Uncle Phineas had ever bought her at the Dollar-a-Pound Overstock Kids' Clothing Store. The store had a boys' and a girls' clothing chute that came down from the ceiling. You punched in your size on a keypad, entered the amount of clothing you wanted in pounds, and pulled a lever. Clothing of all colors plummeted down the chute until your weight designation had been reached. Lots of times Millicent had gotten clothing she really liked this way, but the sweaters tended to be scratchy and smelled of plastic wrap. Millicent examined the label inside the neckline of her new sweater. Cashmere. *Gee whiz*. Even she knew that cashmere was as fancy a fiber as could be knitted. Also in the bag Paisley had left her was a pair of brown, mock-crocodile, high-heeled boots. She got dressed quickly, then went out front to the Winifred T. Langley Memorial Fountain to meet her friends.

She wasn't at the fountain for a full minute when she saw Tonisha and Juanita walking toward her. Evidently they'd been made over by Fiona because they both wore outfits trendier than she'd ever seen on them. Most noticeably, Tonisha's headwrap matched her skirt. Tonisha *never* matched her headwrap to the rest of her outfit because, she'd once said, a matching outfit amounted to conformity. "I will never be a lemming," she'd declared. Furthermore, Millicent saw that Juanita was conspicuously violinless.

Millicent eyed Tonisha and Juanita suspiciously as they approached her.

"Hey, Millicent," they both said in unison.

They seemed guilty or embarrassed, or both.

"Wow, look at you," Tonisha said.

"Yeah, wow," Juanita said.

"You two, too," Millicent said.

The three stood wrapped in an uncomfortable silence.

"Uh," all three said at the same time.

"Listen," they said.

"You first."

"No, you."

"Okay," Tonisha said, "I'll talk." She looked over her shoulder as if she were about to do something illegal. "I . . . uh . . . we are sorry."

"Sorry?" Millicent asked.

"Mmm-hmm," Juanita mumbled, looking over her own shoulder.

"Sorry about what?" Millicent asked. "About deserting me?"

Tonisha cast her eyes downward.

"About betraying me?" Millicent continued. Her voice climbed an octave. She'd rarely, if ever, raised her voice at her friends, but the hurt of being abandoned by them rose up and stuck in her throat like a fish bone, poking her inside until she could only hack out her rage. Her eyes glossed over with tears and her hands locked into fists. "About leaving me high and dry to lead my own one-girl presidential campaign?"

"Yeah, that would be it," Juanita said. Tonisha elbowed her hard and she added, "Ow."

"I don't even know you two anymore," Millicent said. "Just look at you." She swept her arm indicating their outfits.

Tonisha and Juanita stared back at her with deadpan expressions, only their eyes moved, scanning her like surveillance cameras.

Millicent glanced down at her own outfit and thought. *Then, again, maybe my friends aren't the only ones who've gotten carried away.* She looked back up at them sheepishly.

"Well, well," someone said, "what have we here?"

The three of them nearly jumped at the sound of Fiona's voice.

"Tonisha, Juanita, I see you've been following my fashion pointers," Fiona continued. "Tonisha, matching the head thingy to the skirt makes you look taller. And, Juanita, I'm so glad you dumped the fiddle."

Juanita inhaled as if she were about to speak, then pressed her lips closed. Millicent knew Juanita well enough to know that she wanted to correct Fiona for calling her violin a fiddle.

Millicent looked to the other Pretty Liddys who hovered a distance away. Ebi and Heinrich watched Fiona intently, while a red-faced Paisley stared at her feet.

"And I see you're talking to my opponent," Fiona said. Her face morphed from cordial to wicked in a flash. "I can't have that. Bad things can happen to people who talk to my enemies."

"But—" Tonisha blurted.

"Uh—" Juanita grunted.

Fiona circled Millicent like a shark, studying her outfit. "My opponent who is a *cheat*, I might add."

"A cheat?" Tonisha asked.

"Millicent cheated at a—a fashion walk-off?" Juanita asked.

"But that's okay," Fiona continued as if she were the only one speaking. "I've taken care of her cheating ways. In the near future we will all find that You-Can-Dress-Me-Up-but-I'm-Still-a-Geek Girl will return to being Badly Dressed Girl. Almost like Cinderella in reverse." She threw her blond mane back and laughed as she completed her circle around Millicent. She stopped between Millicent and Tonisha and Juanita. "See, I didn't understand how Badly Dressed Girl here could get so fashionable so quickly without a makeover by yours truly. I thought about it and I thought about it and I realized that, really, without the help of a Pretty Liddy, a badly dressed girl had no chance of going through a transformation so dramatic on her own. So I decided to do a little spying early this morning and I found out that a certain little Paisley mouse has been making clothes for Cinderella's presidential ball."

Millicent felt her face flush. She couldn't bring herself to look at Paisley, but she wanted to, desperately.

"Needless to say," Fiona growled, "Paisley will only be designing for *me* from now on."

Millicent still avoided eye contact with Paisley. And she didn't dare look at Fiona.

"So," Fiona continued in an abruptly cheery voice, "now that we all know I'm going to win, shall we go plan my victory party?"

"Let's," Ebi chirped.

"Wonderific," Heinrich said.

"Tonisha? Juanita?" Fiona asked. Glowering subtly at the two of them, she added, "You both look so chic, it would be a shame for you not to be invited to my party."

"Uh, okay," Juanita said, avoiding eye contact with Millicent.

Tonisha nodded, not saying a word.

The Pretty Liddys, and Tonisha and Juanita, turned and merged with a crowd of kids entering the main building like a school of fish riding a current, taking them far away from Millicent.

# Eighteen

**H**istory class hadn't come fast enough for Millicent. She stood by the doorway as students filed in, but Paisley didn't arrive until the bell rang.

"We'll talk later?" Paisley said as she brushed past Millicent.

They went into the classroom and took their respective seats. Millicent tapped her pencil on her desk for the next fifteen minutes, anxious for the part of the class when Mrs. Alpha had everyone get into their research teams. She shifted in her seat, then huffed, then tapped her pencil some more, then tapped her feet, too. Mrs. Alpha had been going on and on about some obscure historical event. Millicent hadn't been paying attention.

"Millicent?" Mrs. Alpha asked.

Millicent froze. She hoped Mrs. Alpha didn't have a tough question in store for her.

"What is all that racket coming from your vicinity?" Mrs. Alpha asked. "It sounds as if you've got the Nicholas Brothers under your desk."

"I'm sorry?" Millicent asked. "I don't know any Nicholas brothers."

"Fayard and Harold Nicholas; Hollywood stars who appeared in over thirty films from the 1930s to '40s. They were tap dancers," Mrs. Alpha said, glaring at Millicent's feet.

"I'm sorry. I'm just excited to work on our history report," Millicent lied. She stopped tapping her feet.

"Oh, yes," Mrs. Alpha said. "Silly me for blabbing on for so long. Class, you may get into your research teams now." She waved the students into motion. Then she added with a wink in Millicent's direction, "You are such a good pupil."

Millicent grinned, though she felt terrible for lying to Mrs. Alpha. Yet she got her wish—she could finally talk to Paisley, who'd just pushed her desk over to be closer to Millicent.

Millicent didn't wait until Paisley sat down. "What happened?" she asked.

Paisley eased into her seat. "This morning? When you came to my house?" she said.

"Yes?"

"Fiona was hiding in the hedges by my front walk," Paisley said.

Millicent winced. "I thought I heard something," she said.

"She saw me put the bag out earlier and she saw you pick it up," Paisley said.

Mrs. Alpha approached, and both Millicent and Paisley whipped out their notebooks and pretended to write. The teacher nodded happily and sauntered past.

"Anyhow," Paisley continued, "Fiona said that she'd make me sorry I ever learned how to thread a sewing machine if I didn't stop making clothes for you."

"Gosh, I'm so sorry," Millicent said.

"Not only that? But I'm not even allowed to speak to you," Paisley said. "Outside of class, I mean."

Millicent scribbled her e-mail address on a slip of paper and pushed it forward. Paisley took it and put it in her skirt pocket.

Millicent pursed her lips crookedly. She sighed. She sighed again. "I guess," she said, "I might have to drop out of the race. I'm not sure how I can win without your help."

"Don't you know anyone who can sew?" Paisley asked.

"No."

"What about shopping? You can go to Don't Even Think About It. And get some designer jeans? They have lots of cool clothes," Paisley suggested

"I—I can't," Millicent said. Though she tried not to show her embarrassment, she thought her face must be bright red.

"Oh," Paisley whispered, "I get it."

Millicent fought back a tear. "So, like I said, I should drop out of the race."

"But you're an inventor. And you're so smart," Paisley said. "Can't you make an invention that'll help you win?"

"You're not the first person to remind me I'm an inventor," Millicent said. "But I'm not a designer. If we could just combine our talents, I'd have it made."

"There must be something . . ." Paisley said.

They both rested their heads on their palms, thinking.

"What about your uncle?" Paisley said. "He invented that thing?"

"What thing?"

"That holographic bell thing," Paisley said.

"Bellhop," Millicent said. She thought about the holographic bellhop and how, with a simple flick of a switch, a metal and fabric armature became a human being with a trick of light. "If only I could create a figment like that on me." Immediately, she gasped.

"What?"

"That's it, that's it!" Millicent nearly shouted.

Paisley put her finger to her lips and shushed her.

"I think I just figured out how you can continue to help me be fashionable yet not get in trouble with Fiona," Millicent said. "You said that you keep your designs on your computer, right?"

"Yeah. I have lots of files."

"Here's my idea." As if she were a spy sharing a matter of national security, Millicent whispered her scheme into Paisley's ear.

# Nineteen

**A**fter school, Millicent rushed home and went straight to the lab, where she found Uncle Phineas working on a new invention.

"Hi, Uncle Phineas," she greeted breathlessly.

"Hi, dear," he said without looking up.

"Uncle Phineas, I have a favor to ask," she said.

He took off his glasses and looked up from his work, only to frown at her when he saw what she was wearing. His eyes scanned down to her feet. "What are *those*?" he asked. His voice teetered on the verge of being loud.

Millicent peered at her feet, suddenly realizing that she'd forgotten to take Paisley's high-heeled boots off. She found herself at a loss for words.

"Those appear to be high heels, yes?" Uncle Phineas said. "And I recall having a conversation with you about the podiatric ramifications of wearing those, yes?"

"Yes, you did tell me they could ruin my feet," Millicent answered.

"Then what are they doing on the ends of your legs?"

Millicent unzipped the boots and popped them off. She sensed that Uncle Phineas wasn't finished with her.

"Where on earth did you get them?" he asked. "And those clothes?" he added, pointing at her outfit.

"Well, the clothes came from the Dollar-a-Pound Overstock Kids' Clothing Store," Millicent fibbed. "Remember? Oh, probably not. We bought twenty pounds of clothing that day." She felt her heart thump against her rib cage.

Uncle Phineas squinted. "And the *shoes*?"

"Remember the girl that came over last week?"

"The fashionable young lady?"

"Paisley."

"Yes, Paisley."

She knew her uncle well enough to know he wouldn't react favorably to the real reason she'd borrowed the shoes in the first place—because they helped her stand a chance of becoming class president—so she decided to lie a little bit. "You see," she began tentatively, "I sort of borrowed them." That part was the truth. Now came the lie. She continued, "Paisley forgot her sneakers for gym today, so we traded. It slipped my mind to return them. You're

177

right. They don't feel good." She grimaced to underscore what Uncle Phineas wanted to hear, hoping this would end the conversation about the shoes.

Uncle Phineas studied her for what seemed like a long time. Finally a smile oozed across his face. "That's my niece. Thoughtful to a fault. She puts her own comfort and health at risk for a friend. Remarkable, yes," he said. He got up and hugged her close. Then he held her at arm's length and locked eyes with her. "You're like a Russian stacking doll, yes? You know the ones? Large, wooden, peanut-shaped dolls with consecutively smaller ones inside," he said.

Millicent nodded. She'd seen them before, but she didn't understand what he meant.

Uncle Phineas continued, "Just when I think I've seen enough of you to make me proud, there's a whole other Millicent inside to make me prouder."

Millicent felt her heart throbbing in her ears. She didn't think he'd take things this far. She thought, at best, he'd say, "All right, they're not yours. Nevertheless, I don't want to see you in high heels ever again," and leave it at that. She hadn't expected him to make her feel guilty.

"Okay," was all she could muster.

Uncle Phineas let his hands slide down her arms,

from her shoulders to her wrists, where he let them linger as if he were taking her pulse.

"You did this all for your friend," he half stated, half asked.

Millicent felt her heart jump, but she said, "Yes." It appeared Uncle Phineas had it partly right. She was a Russian stacking doll, true, but one of lies—one inside another inside another.

Uncle Phineas's eyes looked vacant for a split second, as if he was someplace else mentally. "Very well," he said with a nod. He released her wrists and turned toward his work. "You had a favor to ask me, yes?" he added. He kept his back to her as he talked.

"I was wondering if I could have the holographic bellhop," Millicent said, still puzzled at Uncle Phineas's behavior.

"I suppose so, since I've abandoned it. It can't really handle significant amounts of luggage. So what's the point, yes?" Uncle Phineas said. "It's over there." He pointed over his shoulder with a screwdriver toward the opposite wall.

"Okay, thanks," Millicent said.

"Tell you what," Uncle Phineas said, "I can easily do this upstairs. I'll leave you to your work, yes?" He gathered up the odds and ends he'd been tinkering with, put them in a cardboard box, and left the lab, tromping up the stairs without even a glance in her direction.

Millicent felt as though the air had been sucked out of the room with his exit. It took her a long time to get her breath back.

For the next three days, Millicent tried to keep a low profile at school by avoiding her friends and the Pretty Liddys whenever possible. It wasn't that hard, considering she was barely speaking to her friends anymore, or they were barely speaking to her—it was difficult to say for sure.

After school let out each day, she flew home, changed into her favorite, comfortable clothes, then went to work on her new invention. During her earlier conversation with Paisley, Millicent had realized that she didn't need *actual* clothing to appear fashionable, just the *illusion* of fashionable clothes. For the second walk-off, her "Evening Magic" formal dress wouldn't be real at all. It would be a three-dimensional trick of light. The basis for creating the illusion of a fashionable gown was Uncle Phineas's ditched invention: the holographic bellhop.

She'd begun by removing the human-shaped form from the bellhop's base. She then detached the numerous lenses from the form and set them aside for later.

Next, she installed a computer disk drive into the base.

The information that would go onto the disk is where Paisley's talent came in. She would design an outfit, then photograph it with her digital camera and scan the image into her computer. When she was done, she'd e-mail the file to Millicent, who would then download the image into the holographic bellhop's disk drive.

It took Millicent the full three days to make all the adjustments to the holographic bellhop.

On Thursday, Millicent went directly to the lab after school. All she had left to do was create the garment that would reflect the holographic outfit. She'd cut as much of the reflective fabric from the human-shaped armature as she could. But because the bellhop was smaller than she was, she had only a little fabric to work with. Since she didn't know how to sew she felt at a loss.

She thought about gluing it to something she owned, but what?

Then she remembered the perfect garment for the job. Never mind it didn't belong to her.

# Twenty

**M**illicent crept up to the attic and opened the door at the top of the stairs. Tangerine-colored rays of light from the setting sun shot through the window, illuminating a shower of dust motes. The floor creaked as she made her way to the stack of cardboard boxes across the room.

She pried open what she hoped was the right box. There, on top of a pile of other clothes, lay the girdle. She removed it and sat on the floor. She spread the girdle out flat and took a good long look.

"You seem endlessly fascinated with that thing," Aunt Felicity said from behind her.

Millicent inhaled sharply. "I didn't hear you," she said.

"It's called stealth," Aunt Felicity said, walking toward Millicent. "So what brings you to my underwear this time?"

Millicent didn't know how to explain herself, so she blurted out, "I want it."

"My old underwear?"

"For an invention I'm working on."

"My girdle is going to function as part of an invention?" Aunt Felicity asked. "I'm not so sure I like the idea of a new life for my old underwear. What is the invention? Some sort of springy thing? A little trampoline for pets?"

Millicent stared at her.

"I was never very good at guessing inventions," Aunt Felicity said. "It'd be better to simply tell me what it's going to be."

Millicent continued staring at her, unsure how to respond.

"I get it," Aunt Felicity said. "It's a secret. That's fine. I respect your privacy, but your privacy concerns my private clothing."

"So, it's okay if I use it, then?"

"I didn't say that," Aunt Felicity murmured, then sat cross-legged next to Millicent.

Millicent felt her heart dip. She had to use the girdle.

"You know who made it?" Aunt Felicity asked. She tugged on one leg of the girdle. Without waiting for an answer, she said, "Yup. Pretty Liddy."

Millicent gazed at the girdle intently, admiring its craftsmanship.

"She made it two weeks before the day I was shot through the circus tent," Aunt Felicity said. "Oh, that fateful day. Aside from the years it made me forget, I'll never forget it." She shifted her weight, placed her hand on the floor, and leaned into it.

*A story's coming*, Millicent thought. She pushed the girdle aside so she wouldn't be distracted by it.

"That morning, Pretty Liddy had seemed uncharacteristically friendly. She'd made me fresh-squeezed orange juice and brought it to my private car. 'Felicity,' she'd said, 'I feel it's time to call a truce. Consider this truce juice.' She offered the glass to me but, given that she tried to push me over a waterfall in a barrel, I didn't exactly snatch it out of her hand."

"I understand," Millicent said.

"Nonetheless, she spent an hour in my private car, chatting me up one side and babbling me down the other. After a while, I actually started to soften. We even had a laugh or two. Then she asked if there was any way she could help me prepare for our next show. I said I was fine, but she insisted. 'How about I clean your cannon for you? Last time I looked, it seemed pretty dusty and dirty. We can't have our loveliest and most popular star attraction propelled from a filthy field gun.' She'd worn me down with her charm and her candor, so I said, 'Sure. I'd appreciate that.' She left my car, and later I was shot through the circus tent top."

"Do you think she had something to do with your disappearance?" Millicent asked.

"I can't be sure," Aunt Felicity said. "I have my suspicions, but I suppose they'll be left unproven."

Millicent scratched her head. "Wait a second. If I can prove that Pretty Liddy was responsible for you vanishing, may I have the girdle?"

"Ah, I esteem a good negotiator," Aunt Felicity said.

Millicent went over to an old desk sitting in the corner and found a ballpoint pen and a yellowed sheet of paper. She brought them back to Aunt Felicity. "I have a few questions," she said to her aunt. "Try to answer them to the best of your ability." Then she asked for the measurements of the circus tent, both diameter and height; the length and height of the cannon; the approximate force (in miles per hour) by which Felicity had been shot out of the cannon; the location Felicity should have landed; where she actually went through the tent top; and, finally, Felicity's weight at the time, which Felicity wasn't eager to divulge.

"Really, do I have to provide that bit of information?" Aunt Felicity asked.

"Yes," Millicent said.

Aunt Felicity whispered her weight into Millicent's ear, as if they weren't alone in the attic.

Millicent scribbled numbers and drew lines and arcs until the piece of paper looked as if an ancient Egyptian had doodled hieroglyphics on it while riding in a moving car. "There!" Millicent exclaimed.

"There what?" Aunt Felicity asked.

"My calculations show that the cannon needed to be off by about eight inches for you to have been shot through the tent top," Millicent said. "You wouldn't have felt such a subtle shift, especially from the bottom of the cannon."

"Let me see that." Aunt Felicity slid the paper toward herself. "Hmmm," she continued, "so, you're suggesting that Pretty Liddy changed the trajectory of my cannon."

"Yes." Millicent beamed. She felt proud to have solved Aunt Felicity's greatest mystery.

Aunt Felicity examined the sheet of paper, nodding and ahaing to herself. After a moment she said, "I don't get it. But the calculations are impressive. Even if it's true, though, I still can't prove Pretty Liddy did it," Aunt Felicity said.

"Oh, right," Millicent said. She hadn't accounted for the need for proof. Nonetheless, she thought she'd at least given Aunt Felicity enough reason to let her have the girdle.

Aunt Felicity passed the sheet of paper back to Millicent. "Thanks anyway," she said. "Your theory makes perfect sense."

Millicent raised her eyebrows as if to say, *Are you forgetting something?*

"Yes," Aunt Felicity said, "you may have the girdle."

Millicent grinned and folded the paper up and put it in the pocket of her favorite pants.

# Twenty-one

**M**illicent returned to the lab to assemble what she'd decided to call the Fashionista Girdle.

She went to the time machine.

"Mom and Dad," she said to her parents' picture taped to the door, "I need to use the Millennium Travel Cube."

"For what?" she imagined her mother saying.

"Are you trying to find us?" she pretended her father was asking.

"I need to use it as a dressing room," Millicent said.

"Darn," her father said, "I thought there'd be a family reunion."

"Not this time. But soon, I promise," Millicent said. She meant it, too. One day, she and Uncle Phineas would discover what had gone wrong with the device and would get her parents back.

"Okaaaaay," her parents grumbled.

Millicent opened the door and got in. She tried the

girdle on, but instead of fitting snugly like a pair of cycling shorts, it was as loose on her as a pair of swim trunks. So, she took it off and stapled the sides, taking in excess fabric to make it fit better. Next, she glued the reflective fabric to it with a hot glue gun. Then she punched dozens of tiny holes in the girdle, each hole positioned in strategic correspondence to the lenses in the base of the former holographic bellhop. Finally she strung the lenses from the holographic bellhop through the holes she'd punched in the girdle.

"Is that an invention?" her mother asked.

"Yes," Millicent said.

"Oh, good. What does it do?" her father asked.

Even though she was talking to a photograph, Millicent still felt funny telling her parents what the Fashionista Girdle did. Besides, if her parents were actually around, they would have told her the same thing Uncle Phineas always said: that a worthy invention should make people's lives easier. By that qualification, the Fashionista Girdle was not a commendable invention. It served only Millicent's needs. She decided to stop talking to the photograph.

Besides, the later she stayed up, the more tired she got, and the more tired she got, the more real her conversations with her missing parents seemed.

She'd been working for two hours straight. She rubbed her eyes and checked the lab clock. Then she logged on to her computer to check her e-mail. Nothing. She still hadn't received the design from Paisley.

She also hadn't received Paisley's share of the Masonville Zoo history assignment, which was due tomorrow morning. Because Millicent had spent all her time on the Fashionista Girdle, she would have to complete her share of the assignment in bed. But she felt she could afford to procrastinate. Paisley, she wasn't so sure about.

She returned to the lab table to finish the girdle. Inserting the last lens, she recalled the Masonville Zoo and how Paisley had kept forgetting the camera around her neck. She hoped Paisley hadn't gotten confused about the holographic outfit. She'd gone over the photographic procedure with Paisley several times. "Don't you think you should be taking notes?" Millicent had asked. "No, I'll remember," Paisley had said. Against her better judgment, Millicent had decided not to nag Paisley to write down her instructions. Now she wished she had.

Another check of the lab clock revealed it was midnight—way past her bedtime.

"Come on, Paisley," Millicent whispered.

Just then, her computer announced that she had mail.

"Yes!" she said. She dropped the girdle on the table.

Aunt Felicity called from upstairs, "Your uncle may have approved of your staying up late working on your contraptions, but I do not. It's time you went to bed."

"Just a second," Millicent hollered back. She scrambled to her computer to make sure the e-mail was from Paisley. It was and it had an attachment.

"Now, Millicent," Aunt Felicity shouted.

"I'll be there in a second," Millicent said. She hooked the holographic girdle base up to her computer.

"I'm coming down there," Aunt Felicity shouted.

"Okay, I'm on my way," Millicent said.

Millicent wasn't familiar with her aunt's disciplinary style and she wasn't about to test it. The attachment was entitled Tri-Mension Fashion Designs. "I shouldn't have doubted her," Millicent said to herself. "Looks like she got it right after all." Without opening the attachment, her hand clicked the mouse and her fingers dashed across the keyboard as she set up the file transfer.

She headed for the landing, flicked off the lab lights, and tromped up the stairs to do her homework in bed. Had she looked at her computer screen, she would have seen a series of the most peculiar glittering, purplish, greenish, blackish faces staring back at her like aliens.

# Twenty-two

Millicent slumped into Mrs. Alpha's history class, dragging her feet. Her eyelids hung like old drugstore awnings, which didn't matter because she could barely focus her eyes anyway, she was so tired. She'd stayed up until two in the morning, working on her part of the historical sleuth assignment in bed. She plopped into her seat, laid her head down on her desk, and closed her eyes.

"Attention, class," Mrs. Alpha's voice boomed. Millicent's head jerked upward. "You have fifteen minutes to get into your teams and prepare for your presentations. Chop-chop."

The room filled with the sound of chair legs scraping on the linoleum floor.

"Millicent? Are you okay?" Paisley asked as she swung her desk around.

"I was up late," Millicent mumbled. "Maybe we can do this tomorrow."

"We have to do it today? I helped you and you promised to help me?" Paisley said.

Millicent shook the weariness out of her head. She had given her word to aid Paisley in getting the best grade possible for all she had done for her. Besides, it would have been uncharacteristic for Millicent not to apply herself and get a bad grade. "You're right," she said. "Let's get ourselves an A plus."

They had previously decided that Millicent would do all the talking and Paisley would be in charge of the visuals. They got organized accordingly; Millicent shuffled her papers, Paisley opened up her laptop and some files.

"You scared me last night," Millicent said while she numbered the outline for her talk. "I didn't get your e-mail until late."

"I know. I'm sorry. I had two projects going at the same time? The zoo project and your outfit. It got really confusing," Paisley said.

Millicent nodded. "I know. Don't pay attention to me. I'm just tired."

"Okay, let's start," Mrs. Alpha said. "Why don't we have Roderick and Angus be first with their report on Madame Tournikette's House of Casts?" She gestured for the two of them to come to the front of the classroom.

Roderick did the talking while Angus showed replicas

of the casts they'd seen at Madame Tournikette's. Angus had made them from papier-mâché formed to his own arms and legs. The casts, accompanied by Roderick's graphic details of the famous people's injuries associated with them, garnered plenty of awestruck responses from the students. Millicent couldn't help but feel a little jealous. Roderick and Angus finished their presentation to energetic applause. Millicent hoped for even a fraction of that reception.

Next, the team who'd gotten Princess Dagmar's Castle got up to give their report. They'd built a model of the castle, made entirely of plastic dental floss containers, that opened up at the middle to reveal the inside layout of the fortress. They finished to applause as well.

Next, Mrs. Alpha called on Millicent and Paisley. Millicent sighed. In her gut, she had known they'd be next.

They went to the front of the classrooom and set up their presentation. While Paisley hooked up her laptop to the projection system, Millicent started off.

"The Masonville Zoo," she began, "was founded in 1947 by Buck Inglewood—or Buck I. for short—a nearsighted big game hunter turned animal rights activist." She went on to explain that Buck's career took a turn when he'd borrowed a pair of glasses from a hunting companion. For the first time in his life, he was able to look into an animal's eyes before he shot his gun. He later claimed that the animal, an elephant, stared back at him with an expression so forlorn it seemed to be speaking to him. Buck threw down his rifle, swore off hunting for the rest of his life, and vowed to open a zoo. However, since his only means of making a living had been hunting, he could afford only the most meager variety of animals—keeping a menagerie alive was far different from killing animals. "Thus," Millicent said, "the Masonville Zoo's rather minor offering."

Millicent motioned to Paisley, who gestured for someone to turn off the lights.

"But," Millicent continued, "the Masonville Zoo has its own charms. Take, for example, the pair of yaks, Hepburn and Tracy."

Millicent nodded to Paisley who clicked on her computer's mouse. Immediately, a three-dimensional image of a yak filled the movie screen. With a gentle swipe of the mouse, Paisley made the image rotate until it had made a 360-degree turn. The students made awestruck exclamations.

Mrs. Alpha clapped her hands, and Millicent grinned at Paisley.

Millicent covered the other exhibits: the zebra, the elephant, the otter, chimpanzee, and rhino. Each creature was depicted in a three-dimensional image onscreen, and each got an astonished response from every student. Millicent could tell that with every picture Paisley felt more confident that she'd be getting a good grade, which made Millicent feel as though she'd returned Paisley's favors.

"And now we've reached the final exhibit," Millicent read from her notes. "Mr. Ento's Bugopolis." She turned the page and continued to read. "The Bugopolis was originally a gas station and insect zoo until 1945, when Buck Inglewood bought it."

Paisley brought up a picture of the old gas station, then she brought up a picture of the current Bugopolis.

"'Coleoptera' is the scientific name for beetles," Millicent said. "It means 'sheath winged.' Our foray into Bugopolis will focus on this remarkable insect."

A few students, mostly boys, whispered, "cool."

Paisley clicked her mouse. At first, the class didn't respond. Then, one by one, the students started to murmur in disappointment.

"What's that?" a boy asked.

"Oh, man, that's not a bug," a boy sitting in the front row said. He huffed and folded his arms.

"Maybe it's Fashionopolis, not Bugopolis," another girl said.

"Oh," Paisley said, "I must have gotten mixed up?" She clicked her mouse, searching among her files.

Millicent looked up to see a lime-green-and-violet floral-print dress on the screen. It had layers of fabric on the torso, sculpted around the front like a wrapper on a candy. It had a floor-length skirt as full and as frothy as the foam on a hot chocolate. It rotated slightly before disappearing off the screen.

"I'm sorry?" Paisley said. "I'll find the right picture?" She fumbled around for a few seconds while the class gradually lost focus on Millicent's and Paisley's report. "I can't find it? I don't know where it is?"

Although she knew she wasn't being completely fair, Millicent found herself wishing she hadn't entrusted Paisley with the responsibility of the visual presentation aspect of their project. The pictures taken in Bugopolis could have been so sensational as to give both of them an A, or even an A+. Exasperated, Millicent dropped her arms to her sides. Her notes fluttered down to the floor. She'd always been a straight-A student. She looked out the classroom window and wondered what else could go wrong. She was so upset she didn't realize that the worst that could go wrong already had.

# Twenty-three

**B**ackstage at the second presidential fashion walk-off, Millicent stood in the dark in an old dance unitard and the Fashionista Girdle. "Okay, kids," she heard Mr. Pennystacker say, "today's theme is Evening Magic. Your presidential candidates will be modeling formal attire. First up is Fiona Dimmet." The music exploded, but it wasn't nearly as loud as the sound of the students cheering as they watched Fiona do her walk.

Millicent had caught a glimpse of Fiona's dress before she took to the runway. Made of a shimmery fabric, it swirled like a cyclone with every step she took. Millicent pictured the faces of the kids in attendance. They must be thinking Fiona looked fantastic.

She decided to peek out to see Fiona's walk. She went over to the curtains and parted them just in time to see Fiona marching back toward the stage, a look of supreme triumph on her face. She saw Millicent and her eyes went narrow and she smirked. "I win," she mouthed.

Millicent clamped the curtains shut. How could Fiona be so smug? She thought she'd put an end to Paisley designing for Millicent, but she had underestimated the inventor. Millicent felt her neck get hot, then her face, and finally, the top of her head. "I'll show her," she said. She got onto the holograph base and grabbed the remote control in preparation for her entrance.

"Yay, Fiona," Mr. Pennystacker said over the sound system. "Man, wasn't that gown absolutely *spectabulous*?" The students went hysterical with applause and cheers. Then, almost offhandedly, he said, "Next, we have Millicent Madding."

Millicent flicked a switch on the remote control and the base whirred into action. "I hope my outfit is as pretty as the one Paisley accidentally showed earlier," she whispered to herself. She flicked the joystick on the Fashionista Girdle's remote and glided through the space between the curtains.

*Oh, no!* she realized, *the dress Paisley showed in history class was my dress!*

If Paisley wasn't able to find the picture of the coleoptera—the big iridescent beetle from Mr. Ento's Bugopolis—then what had been downloaded into the Fashionista Girdle?

She looked at the base as it, and she, rolled down the runway.

"Oh, my goodness!" she shouted. From her waist to her feet, she saw a glossy mass, an insect's abdomen. On her sides, six legs protruded from the insect's thorax, like wicked, twisted chopsticks.

Mr. Pennystacker barked, then ducked behind the red velvet curtain.

Several girls in the front row screamed at the tops of their lungs and ran toward the exits. Some boys jumped up, waving their fists as if they'd take on the giant bug, then promptly ran out of the auditorium, too. The remaining students stood up and backed away to the rear of the room.

Millicent fiddled with the joystick on the remote control until she got the base to turn around. In full throttle, she zoomed toward the gap between the curtains. She glanced into the wings and saw Paisley, whose hands were clapped to her mouth and whose eyes were bulging, then Millicent burst backstage.

She turned off the Fashionista Girdle and got off the base to catch her breath.

"Well," Mr. Pennystacker's voice boomed over the sound system, "that was something. I suppose we don't even have to take a vote on the second walk-off. I pronounce Fiona Dimmet the winner! There's only one more walk-off to go and its theme is Fantasy Fashion. Next Friday, you will choose a president, though I think we all know who it'll be. See you then."

With one more walk-off to go, Millicent thought she might as well give up now. As grateful as she was to Paisley, she could no longer count on her talents to make her fashionable and she couldn't risk getting Paisley in any more trouble with Fiona. Worse, she didn't have any cool clothes of her own, other than the ones Paisley had already made her and which everyone had already seen, and she couldn't afford to buy any chic outfits. At that moment, her political aspirations all but died.

Millicent felt a tear form in the corner of her eye, a hot, salty pest of a thing that threatened to burn a trail down her cheek. She wiped it away before it embarrassed her more than she was already.

# Twenty-four

For several days the following week, Millicent felt as though redemption was a long way off. Everywhere she went on the Winifred T. Langley Middle School campus, she was greeted with exclamations of, "Look, it's a bug, it's a girl; it's Bug Girl," or "Quick, get the bug spray." Some kids took one look at her, fell into a fit of convulsions and mock screams, then ran, only to collapse into laughter a few yards away. Other kids had taken it upon themselves to make crudely drawn campaign posters, which they'd taped over Millicent's own, depicting a large blackish beetle with braids. A red circle with a slash mark through it was drawn over the insect. VOTE HUMAN, the posters read.

Her friends hadn't behaved too badly toward her, considering they still worked for Fiona's campaign. Every time Tonisha saw Millicent, she'd whisper, "I'm so sorry." Once, Juanita saw Millicent and, after checking to see if Fiona was nearby, said, "If I had my violin, I'd play you a mournful piece, like Bach's Sonata for Violin and Piano, Part 7." Pollock saw her and said, "I want to capture your forlorn face in a painting." Then he added, "After the election." Roderick wasn't any more polite than he ever was. Each day, when he saw her in history class, he said, "I wish I could give you the A I got on the historical sleuth assignment," which Millicent could tell he didn't mean. Then, he'd add, "And I'm so sorry you were mistaken for a bug in that embarrassing walk-off episode," which Millicent could tell he also didn't mean.

Leon Finklebaum stood alone as the friend who hadn't forsaken her. He walked her to her classes whenever possible and he continued to have lunch with her. "I thought you made a great coleoptera," he'd said to her over sandwiches at the Winifred T. Langley Memorial Fountain.

Now, the day before the final walk-off, Millicent and Leon sat together again at the fountain.

"I get sleepy after I eat," Leon said. He unwrapped his sandwich and folded the wax paper into a neat square. Millicent smiled and he chuckled. "But I guess I'm almost always sleepy."

Millicent unwrapped her meal. The Robotic Chef had made her a tuna and peanut butter sandwich. She separated the two pieces of bread, trying to keep the tuna on one slice and the peanut butter on the other.

"Leon?" Millicent asked.

"Yeah?"

"Tomorrow is the last walk-off."

"I know."

"You haven't said anything about it."

Leon set his sandwich on his lap. "You know how I feel about this whole fashion business," he said. "It has nothing to do with being a good class president. It certainly has nothing to do with winning an election."

"But it's about fashion now, Leon," Millicent said.

"Have you forgotten why you wanted to be president in the first place?" he asked.

Millicent hadn't forgotten why she wanted to be president, really. Well, sort of. In a way. "Now, becoming class president is about being stylish and pretty and walking well," she said. "The rules have changed, Leon."

"Have they?" Leon asked with a mouthful of food. "And if they have, who says they can't be changed back again?"

Millicent shook her head. She wondered if his good nature was a Tweedledum to the Tweedledee of his naïveté—they seemed to go tumbling over each other until she couldn't tell if he was being optimistic or dim.

She couldn't single-handedly change the rules back to the usual ones by which class presidents were elected. Too many people had been hypnotized into believing that being fashionable was the same as being presidential. A tide that large could not be turned by an individual. Especially by an individual named Millicent Madding.

"Oh, Leon," was all she managed to say.

She wanted to tell him about her plan to win the next walk-off, but she knew he wouldn't understand. Besides, she knew she couldn't risk revealing her secret weapon too soon.

"Anyway," he said, "even if you win the next walk-off, won't that put you neck and neck with Fiona? Won't you have to do another sort of tiebreaker walk-off?"

Millicent nearly gagged on her sandwich. She hadn't thought about what would happen if she won. Suddenly she wished Leon were right: that the rules could be changed back to the original, sane, fair ones.

Friday came and the auditorium was once again filled to capacity. Millicent waited backstage, this time with nothing more than a grocery store paper bag. The theme for the final walk-off was Fantasy Fashion, which meant that Fiona and Millicent were to wear over-the-top styles like those shown by European designers. The theme, like the other two, had been Ebi's idea. Millicent didn't know what Fiona would be wearing, but she felt confident that what she had in her bag would outshine anything Fiona had. Millicent peeked out between the curtains.

She saw a number of Fiona groupies in the front row. They'd made FIONA DIMMET FOR PRESIDENT posters, attached them to sticks, and were waving them. She looked at their feet. The girls were wearing high heels and the boys were wearing Heinrich Putzkammery bright sneakers. "Fabulistic Fiona," they shouted. Some girls had the tips of their hair dyed different colors, like Ebi Sato's.

Also in the front row, Tonisha sat with Juanita, Pollock, and Roderick. Tonisha and Juanita had on high heels, like the other girls, and Roderick wore a vivid purple bow tie. Pollock was dressed in his usual paint-splattered clothes, but had his hair spiked like Heinrich's.

A couple of rows back, Leon waved his own handmade sign. VOTE FOR MILLICENT, it read. PLEASE.

"Thanks, Leon," Millicent whispered. She returned to her corner backstage and started to get dressed in her secret outfit.

Mr. Pennystacker took to the stage in a surprisingly

nimble move. "Hey, all. Like the duds?" he shouted into the microphone at the podium.

The crowd cheered.

"Yeah, I'm stylin'," he answered. He tugged at the lapels of his khaki blazer to reveal his chartreuse shirt and cobalt-blue-and-hot-pink-striped tie. "All right, let's get this show on the road. Today's walk-off determines your next class president. The theme is Fantasy Fashion—in which the theatrical and the stylish meet in a head-on fashion collision! Let's hear it for your first contender, Fiona Dimmet!"

The students roared. The lights went down, the music went up, and out stepped Fiona into the spotlight's bright pool. The students gasped when they saw her, then went into a rippling of "wow" and "cool."

Millicent stumbled toward the gap between the curtain to get a look at her. "Wow," Millicent echoed.

Fiona had on a dress covered in crystals that caught beams from the spot, refracting them into dueling swords of light. She looked like a mad chandelier. She tromped down the runway, sending shards of light this way and that, got to the end, stopped, and put her hands on her hips. Then she spun around and flounced up the runway.

Millicent closed the curtain before Fiona saw her.

The crowd went into a frenzy.

The lights went up and, after a moment, Mr. Pennystacker's voice came over the sound system. "Brilliant," he said. "That was Fiona Dimmet, kids. I guess formality calls for our next candidate, though that act is indisputably hard to follow. At any rate, I present to you Millicent Madding." He went to the curtains and stuck his head between them. "Give it a shot, Millicent. The worst you can do is try."

The lights went back down and the music got louder. Millicent took a deeper than deep breath, then plunged onto the stage.

# Twenty-five

It took a second for Millicent's eyes to adjust to the bright light. But that second felt like forever—as though she'd been shot out of a cannon and was soaring above the student body. She felt floaty and special and as if she'd already been elected president or crowned princess, or both. She blinked, then started walking.

At first, the students gasped collectively, then they broke into ear-shattering yells. "Fabulistic!" they screamed. "Spectabulous!"

Millicent focused on keeping one booted foot in front of the other, and her face bored looking, though her giddiness made her feel as if she would fall.

Heinrich bolted from the sidelines toward the runway and started snapping pictures of Millicent. "Give me megapouty," he said.

Millicent glanced at him and extended her lower lip.

"Marvelatious!" he cried, then took another picture.

"Now give me sly."

Millicent grinned a slanted grin at him.

He took another picture. "Now give me angry, fuming. Pretend a mean monster is going to take your pretty shoes." He growled and lunged at her, acting as if he were grabbing at her feet. "Grrrrr! I'm coming to take your pretty shoes!" he said.

Millicent glowered at him.

"Beautilicious!" Heinrich shouted.

"What is going on out there?" Fiona shrieked from the wings. She bounded onstage, saw Millicent, and grabbed her chest in shock. "Ah, ah, ah," she gasped. As if she were performing a Shakespearean death scene, she staggered to maintain her balance, tangling herself up in the velvet curtain. Ebi ran out and clutched her by the elbow to hold her up. "I'd recognize that workmanship anywhere! The line, the color use, the fabulisticness! It's an original Pretty Liddy design!" she screamed.

And it was.

Millicent's secret fashion weapon was none other than Aunt Felicity's stretchy, human cannonball unitard. She'd gone to the attic on Monday after school and had put the whole costume into a paper bag, except the helmet, which she thought would be more of an encumbrance than a help. Then she smuggled the ensemble out of the attic, as if she were kidnapping it, which was not that far from the truth since she didn't ask Aunt Felicity's permission to borrow it. She brought it to her room and laid it out on her bed. It looked funny—long and skinny—as if it were hungry for her to try it on, so she did. She was happy to find that it fit her like a swimsuit would. She kept the costume in her room all week until Friday, when she brought it to school and hid it backstage for the walk-off.

Now the costume seemed to be carrying her down the runway with its winged boots. She got to the end of the ramp and untied the cape. She did a spin, swinging the cape like a matador, to the cheers of the kids.

"Spin it, work it!" Heinrich shouted as he wildly clicked photos of her.

"This isn't fair," Fiona yelled. Ebi clutched her elbow tighter.

Paisley came from the wings and stood behind Fiona, clapping silently.

Millicent trotted back up the runway, keeping full eye contact with Fiona. She felt more than strong enough to withstand her glare.

Mr. Pennystacker rushed to center stage, taking both Fiona and Millicent by the hand, one on either side of him. "This has been an amazing competition," he hollered over the crowd. "Who will be your next president? Fiona Dimmet?" He raised her hand and the students cheered. "Or Millicent Madding?" He raised Millicent's hand and the students cheered even louder. "That settles it. Millicent Madding is your new fashionable class president!"

The students went wild, and Millicent herself started to cheer until Leon's voice rang in her head. *Besides,* he had said at lunch Thursday, *even if you win the next walk-off, won't that put you neck and neck with Fiona? Won't you have to do another sort of tiebreaker walk-off?* Her heart plummeted past her stomach toward the winged boots she had on.

The whole presidential election was starting to feel like an endless nightmare. Suddenly she wanted it all over with. She hoped that no one would notice that another walk-off was needed. She hoped that she could fulfill her presidential duties, like arranging bake sales and setting up car washes to fund student activities. She hoped the auditorium would empty and everyone would get back to their lives as if the Pretty Liddys had never come to Winifred T. Langley Middle School—as if Pretty Liddy's Junior Fashion Academy had remained just a strange little school on the other side of town. She hoped to go home and put Aunt Felicity's human cannonball outfit back in a box with mothballs and pretend she'd never worn it.

As gently as she could manage, she freed herself from Mr. Pennystacker's grasp and inched her way to the wings.

Then, as shrill as a whistle, Fiona's voice rose above the crowd. "HEY, WAIT A SECOND!" she screamed.

# Twenty-six

Saturday morning passed with Millicent spending most of it in bed thinking about the tiebreaker walk-off. Mr. Pennystacker had scheduled it for Monday because he said that he couldn't wait until Friday to have a class president and neither could the student body. After Fiona's outburst, Mr. Pennystacker had announced the theme, Free Choice, Free Style—Ebi had whispered it in his ear—for which the candidates were to wear their favorite outfits. Millicent didn't have a clue as to how she'd compete in the final round, especially on such short notice. She'd run out of options.

Lunchtime came and she still lay in bed, facedown. Madame Curie jumped up onto Millicent's back and sat on her shoulders.

"Stop, M.C.," she said. "I'm in a lousy mood." She rolled over and the cat leaped off the bed and ran for the closet. The door was open and she went inside.

"Millicent?" Aunt Felicity called from the hallway. She knocked on the bedroom door.

Millicent jumped up and snatched the bag that contained her aunt's human cannonball costume and shoved it under her bed. Then she flopped onto bed so that she landed on her stomach. "Yeah?" she said into her pillow.

"Are you all right?"

"Yeah."

"I'm coming in," Aunt Felicity said, then opened the door.

Unlike Uncle Phineas, Aunt Felicity announced herself before entering instead of asking permission. Uncle Phineas would request clearance at least one time, maybe two or three times, before turning the knob. And even then he'd stick his head in to make sure he was allowed to enter. Millicent wished her aunt were a smidgen more like her uncle.

"Okay," Millicent answered, but Aunt Felicity was already several steps inside her room.

"It's nearly lunch," Aunt Felicity said. "The Robotic Chef made macaroni and cheese. Only the part that's supposed to be cheesy doesn't smell like cheese. It smells like vanilla custard."

"It is vanilla custard," Millicent said. The Robotic

Chef had made it exactly the same way once, before Aunt Felicity's return. Millicent actually liked the dish. To her, it didn't seem that far off from rice pudding, which she enjoyed by the scoopful. "It's pretty good with whipped cream and a dash of cinnamon," she added.

Aunt Felicity sauntered over to the window and swung the curtains open, then she took a seat on the edge of the bed. "What is this all about?" she asked. "You've stayed in bed entirely too long."

Millicent rolled onto her side. "Have you ever exhausted your alternatives?" she asked.

"Goodness, of course," Aunt Felicity said. "When I first found myself homeless on the streets of Pinnimuk City. I actually tried to find work, but having lost my memory of a completely impractical career, I was unemployable. For many days I had no money and nothing to eat."

"What did you do?" Millicent asked, sure her aunt had been imaginative in finding a way out.

"I told the truth," Aunt Felicity said.

Millicent sighed. She'd expected a more interesting solution.

"I went to the nearest Sisters of Routine Kindnesses and Involuntary Thoughtfulnesses Mission and told them my story. They helped me out," Aunt Felicity said.

It seemed to Millicent that telling the truth was over-rated. Not that she felt lying was better. She simply felt that the truth had barely any flash or zip. She needed an invention. Compared to a gadget, the truth was remarkably lackluster. Besides, she didn't think the truth would work for her circumstance. What was the truth about her situation, anyway? That she was a bad dresser by nature? Standing up in front of the student body of Winifred T. Langley Middle School and confessing that she dressed poorly wouldn't win her the presidency.

As if Aunt Felicity could read her thoughts, she said, "You'd be surprised how liberating the truth can be."

"My problem is not the kind that telling the truth will change," Millicent said.

"You never know," Aunt Felicity said. She stood up and accidentally kicked the paper bag under the bed. A winged boot fell out. She picked the boot up and put it back in the bag. "Speaking of the truth . . ."

"I borrowed your human cannonball costume," Millicent said. "I'm sorry for not telling you and for not asking permission." Like an uncapped fire hydrant, she let the whole story gush from her mouth. She told her aunt about how Fiona had changed the election rules for class president, how Fiona had given Mr. Pennystacker and others makeovers, how her friends had deserted her, and how she tied one walk-off and won another. She told her aunt about Paisley's help and the Fashionista Girdle and the smashing success the human cannonball costume had been. Finally, she told her aunt that the last walk-off was Monday and that she had no more fashionable ensembles to wear. She leaned back on her pillow and heaved a sigh.

"See?" Aunt Felicity said. "Telling the truth can be a relief." Without a further word, she rose and walked out of the room.

She could use the relief that the truth could bring, but what was the truth? She thought long and hard about it. Then it dawned on her that the truth didn't always sparkle. Sometimes, the truth was dressed plainly and you might pass it by for a prettier lie. But the truth radiated heart. With that in mind, she got out of bed to work on her campaign speech.

# Twenty-seven

Monday morning arrived, cold and blustery, blowing leaves against Millicent's bedroom window.

Millicent buttoned her coat while Madame Curie wound a figure eight around her ankles. "Is that your way of wishing me luck, M.C.?" Millicent asked. She picked up Madame Curie and touched noses with her. "Thanks, but I'm beyond luck. I'm losing an election today." The cat licked her nose. "No, really. My luck has run out." She put the cat down and went downstairs for breakfast.

Uncle Phineas was in the kitchen talking into the Robotic Chef's microphone. "Eggs, sunny-side up, please," he enunciated. He saw Millicent and said, "Good morning. I'm hoping that I get eggs this morning, yes? The last time I asked for eggs sunny-side up, I got a slice of quiche doused in hot sauce." He tapped on the Robotic Chef's microphone. "This thing's a bit like culinary Russian roulette, yes?"

The two of them hadn't talked much since he'd caught her wearing high heels. In fact, this was the most he'd said to her in many days.

Millicent giggled—less because of Uncle Phineas's joke than the fact that he was talking to her. She didn't know what else to say, so she added, "Yeah, you can never be sure what it'll serve you." After an awkward silence, she continued, "I'm just having cereal and I'm getting it myself." She went to the refrigerator and got a carton of milk.

"I'm glad to see you're not wearing those podiatric monstrosities," Uncle Phineas said.

Once again, Millicent found herself wanting to tell him the truth about why she'd worn the high heels, but she couldn't bring herself to do it. Instead, she said, "Me, too."

"I'm still waiting for you to tell me the truth about those shoes," he said.

"What?" Millicent heard herself ask.

"The truth about the shoes. I've been waiting several days to hear it," he said.

The truth? Why was the subject of truth poking its head up here and there, like a prairie dog in the field of her life? Everyone seemed to want the truth from her. And how did he know she'd lied to him?

"I bet you're wondering how I knew you lied," he said. Millicent felt her face go red and she nodded. "Remember when I asked you why you were wearing high heels and then clasped your wrists?"

"Yes."

"It was a tad deceptive on my part, but I was feeling your pulse," Uncle Phineas said. "It jumped when you lied, yes? That's how I knew."

"Oh," Millicent said. *Of course. The old pulse trick.*

"Hurt my feelings that you'd lie to me," he said.

"I'm sorry," she said. She hadn't intended to hurt his feelings.

"So, why the shoes?"

Since she'd been revealed, Millicent told Uncle Phineas her story in the same way she'd told it to Aunt Felicity. She went into particular detail about how she'd been transformed into a beetle in front of the whole student body.

"Coleoptera!" he exclaimed. "Which kind?"

"Scarabaeidae," Millicent said.

"The lovely scarab beetle, yes?" he said. "All pretty and shiny and twinkly—"

"Uncle Phineas," Millicent whined.

"Sorry," he said. "Go on."

Millicent continued her story, getting to the part where Mr. Pennystacker rescheduled the tiebreaker walk-off for this morning, but Uncle Phineas interrupted. "You know," he said, "that Fashionista Girdle does not qualify as a worthy invention. It didn't help anyone except you. You understand that, do you not?"

"Yes, I do."

"Just making sure."

Millicent started to talk, but Uncle Phineas interrupted again. "And, you know," he said, "that a fashion walk-off to decide a class president is absurd, yes?"

"Well . . ." Millicent said.

"It is."

"But Fiona gave Mr. Pennystacker and a bunch of other kids makeovers, and pretty soon almost everyone wanted makeovers and they didn't care about what really mattered. Even my friends stopped behaving like themselves. It is as if they have been hypnotized."

"It reminds me of that silly movie in which aliens took over Pinnimuk City by—"

"*The Incursion of the Gray Matter Snatchers from Planet Zilthon,*" Millicent said.

"That's the one," Uncle Phineas said.

Millicent looked at the kitchen clock. "I guess I'd better go, or I'll be late," she said.

"Wait! So, what about the election?" Uncle Phineas asked.

Millicent stood up. "I suppose I'll have to lose gracefully today," she said.

"That's it?" Uncle Phineas asked with an astonished ring to his voice.

Millicent walked over to the kitchen counter and said to the Robotic Chef, "Millicent's lunch, please." The chef's metal arm opened the refrigerator, removed a paper bag, and dropped it on the floor. She picked it up, walked back to her uncle, and set the bag down on the kitchen table.

"I'm going to lose anyway," Millicent said. "I have nothing but my favorite clothes on and they're not expensive or fancy or even *nearly* stylish. They're my favorite clothes. That's all." She looked down at her tattered sneakers. They weren't like her new ones. They knew the curves of her feet. "What else do I have?" she added.

"What else do you have?" Uncle Phineas asked. He stood up and continued, his voice louder, "What else do you have?" He paced the kitchen like an agitated animal. "You, dear niece, have everything. You're smart, you're clever, you're endearing, you're a hard worker, and if you gave yourself half a chance, you'd be an inspiring leader. Those are a few of the things you have. That's the truth."

"Those things don't matter anymore. The rules have changed," Millicent said. She'd heard herself make that statement to Leon before. She hoped her uncle wouldn't give her a similar retort to the one Leon had, but she had her suspicions.

Uncle Phineas said, "Change them back."

"You don't understand, Uncle Phineas," she said. She was getting tired of saying this. "I can't reverse the rules. I have to go." She turned away so she wouldn't have to look him in the eye, and left the kitchen without her lunch.

# Twenty-eight

Lunchtime came around faster than Millicent would have liked. She went to her locker, only to remember that she'd forgotten her lunch. She checked her wallet, then all the compartments in her backpack, then her pockets for money. She had none. However, she found the sheet of paper with the calculations she had done to prove that Aunt Felicity's cannon had been tampered with. It was interesting, but it wasn't money. And it wouldn't buy her lunch. She folded it up and put it back in her pocket. Her belly gurgled and she closed her eyes. To lose an election on an empty stomach made her queasier than she already felt. She shut her locker door with a sigh.

Millicent decided to head straight for the auditorium to wait for the inevitable. She went into the lobby. She heard the Pretty Liddys' voices talking with a woman whose voice she didn't recognize. As quietly as she could, she ducked behind an open door and peered through the crack into the auditorium, cupping her ear so she could eavesdrop effectively.

"How are you feeling?" the woman asked Fiona.

"Great. Ready," Fiona answered.

The woman's back was to Millicent. Still, Millicent saw that she had on a snazzy suit made of a multicolored tweed fabric. She wore blisteringly pink high-heeled shoes, and her hat was as big as a patio umbrella. Millicent thought she might be the same woman she'd seen at the Mighty Masonville Mall's fashion show, which now seemed years ago.

The woman put her hands on her hips. "Good," she said, "show these Langley bumpkins how we do it at Pretty Liddy's Junior Fashion Academy."

"Fabulistically," Heinrich said.

"That's right," the woman said. She turned to walk away, but stopped when Ebi addressed her.

"Excuse me," Ebi said. "Miss Pretty Liddy?"

The woman spun on her heels. "Yes?" she answered.

Millicent nearly yelped and blew her cover. *Pretty Liddy,* she thought. *Oh, my gosh.* She pressed her palm over her mouth.

"How does Fiona's makeup look?" Ebi asked.

"Gorgeoustic," Pretty Liddy said. She scanned down

Fiona's person, her eyes landing on her feet. "But your shoes . . ."

Fiona looked worried. "Are they wrong?" she asked.

"Wrong?" Pretty Liddy blasted. "Unquestionably!"

Fiona slipped them off and gestured for Ebi to bring her new ones. Ebi ran backstage. Fiona dabbed at the corner of her eye as if a tear had threatened to smudge her makeup.

"I'm sorry," Pretty Liddy said. "I'm not mad at you. I'm mad at the shoes."

Millicent heard students approaching, so she got out from behind the door and tried to appear as nonchalant as possible, pretending to pick a piece of lint off her sleeve. The students started to file into the auditorium.

"I'll be watching," Pretty Liddy said to Fiona, then took a seat in the last row.

Millicent took a deep breath. Not only did Millicent have to accept loss, she had to accept it in front of her aunt's nemesis. It seemed to be a cruel kind of inheritance.

Mr. Pennystacker boarded the stage with his now characteristic pluckiness. Millicent watched from the wings, wiping her clammy palms on her pants. She liked Mr. Pennystacker's ensemble: a dark blue suit with an orange shirt and a pistachio-colored tie. "Well, kids," he said, "today's the day you decide on your new class president." The audience cheered in response. "The fashion theme is Free Choice, Free Style, which means the candidates have chosen their favorite outfits—day or dressy—to model. Let's hear it for your first candidate, Fiona Dimmet!"

The lights dimmed and the music got louder until the floor vibrated. Fiona came out between the curtains with a vengeance, and the Pretty Liddys in the front row cheered. She paused before heading down the runway and whipped her long hair so hard it traveled around the back of her head and hit her in the face. "Ow," she whispered.

Only Millicent heard her. She wanted to giggle. It had been a long while since she'd been tempted to laugh, but she thought it better not to.

Fiona wore a ensemble consisting of a brightly colored top with a little yellow cotton jacket, designer jeans, and strappy shoes. Even at her most casual she still put her outfits together better than Millicent.

Fiona pranced down the runway like a pony, frowning as if she were wearing a bridle and a bit. Heinrich ran up to the ramp to take pictures of her. "Give me poutalicious!" he shouted. Fiona faced the camera and extended her lower lip and arched an eyebrow. Heinrich snapped a couple of shots, then disappeared.

Fiona got to the end of the runway, did her usual pause and turn, then headed for the curtain. The kids roared and Fiona took a bow.

The lights came up and Mr. Pennystacker spoke into the microphone. "Fashionabulous," he said. "That was Fiona Dimmet. Oh, exhilarating." He stopped to catch his breath. "Now, we have Millicent Madding." He motioned for someone to dim the lights, but Millicent came onstage and took the microphone from him.

"No need to turn the lights down," Millicent said. "And forget the music. I won't be walking."

The room became deathly still, as if the oxygen had been sucked out of it.

"I—uh—I—" Millicent stuttered.

A Pretty Liddy girl in the front row snickered.

"I—well, I—" Millicent stammered.

"Booooo," a girl hollered.

"You're not a fashionista," another girl yelled.

Something in Millicent's head clicked, and suddenly she felt something like courage rise from her gut. For an instant, she didn't want to give up without a fight— without being honest. She decided to go with the sensation. She reached into her pocket and pulled out the speech she'd written.

"You're right," she said. "I'm not a fashionista." She scanned the audience and her gaze caught Leon's. Safe, supportive Leon. Leon who believed in her. "Yeah," she continued, "I'm not a fashionista. I'm me."

Leon grinned as wide as he could at her.

She unbuttoned her coat and let it fall to the floor, then she unfolded her speech. "This is how I dress," she read. "These are my favorite pants. I didn't get them in a fancy store like Don't Even Think About It, or A Week's Salary. I got them at Dollar-a-Pound Overstock Kids' Clothing Store." Fiona giggled, but Millicent ignored her. "I know many of you are familiar with the store because I've seen you there." A few kids shifted uncomfortably in their seats. "Anyway, these pants may not be the very latest thing, but I like them," she continued. "They're comfortable and they're soft because they've been washed so many times. They're like friends." The crowd was quiet, especially the Wunderkinder, whose eyes were downcast, so she continued. "My top was given to me by an acquaintance of my uncle's. I didn't even pick it out myself, so I had to *learn* to like it. A lot of things in life are like that. You have to learn to like them."

She took a step forward and moved the microphone closer to her mouth.

"You might learn to like me as president if you give me a chance," she said, "because I'll work hard for all of you."

Her mind flashed on Uncle Phineas. He'd said she was a hard worker that very morning. She remembered what else he'd said about her. She lifted her eyes from her speech. "I'm smart, clever, endearing, and I could be an inspiring leader. Someone who loves me said I was those things, so maybe he was being partial, but I think those are qualities you would want in a class president. I don't think you need a president who can wear make-up well or walk well or pout well."

A few kids murmured in agreement.

"Anyhow, that's all I have to say," she stated. She folded up her speech, picked up her coat, handed Mr. Pennystacker the microphone, and walked off the stage. In silence, she made her way up the center aisle to the entrance of the auditorium, then went outside. She headed for the Winifred T. Langley Memorial Fountain.

She felt dizzy. She hadn't had lunch and she'd just given the most difficult speech of her life. She wanted to sit down.

A clack of footsteps pelted the air.

"Millicent," Aunt Felicity called.

"You forgot your lunch," Uncle Phineas shouted.

231

Millicent stopped in her tracks, then turned around. Her aunt and uncle caught up to her and wrapped her up like a gift in their arms.

"We heard your speech," Aunt Felicity said.

Millicent sighed with relief at seeing their faces. "But I probably won't win," she said.

"Doesn't matter, yes?" Uncle Phineas said. "You told the truth and you single-handedly restored the rules."

"I guess so," Millicent said.

The bell rang and students started filing out of the school.

Aunt Felicity and Uncle Phineas straightened themselves up.

"I'm hungry," Millicent said, and all three of them laughed.

# Twenty-nine

Millicent sat at the Winifred T. Langley Memorial Fountain with Uncle Phineas and Aunt Felicity, eating her sandwich and watching her classmates drift out of the building. A few of them waved at her and some even stopped to tell her she'd given a great speech. Most of the students, though, scarcely acknowledged her or walked by without so much as looking at her.

"You guys can go home, now," Millicent said to her aunt and uncle. She stared at the exit. More kids filed out.

"We'll stay until you're done," Aunt Felicity said.

"No, really, you can go home," Millicent said, her eye still on the door. Thankfully, the person she was keeping watch for hadn't left yet. If she could only get her aunt and uncle to leave, she might be able to avoid a scene. She'd been through enough that day already.

"What are you trying to hide from us?" Aunt Felicity asked.

"Nothing," Millicent answered. She watched the doorway. Suddenly a big hat appeared. It spanned the width of the doorway. Millicent shoved her unfinished sandwich in her lunch bag. "Okay," she blurted. "Time to go."

"Most peculiar, yes?" Uncle Phineas said.

"You haven't finished your lunch," Aunt Felicity said.

"Whoooo, I'm stuffed," Millicent said. She patted her stomach and stood.

"But I made you cookies. Well, the Robotic Chef did. They're supposed to be peanut butter cookies, but they smell like Thai food. Red curry, I think," Aunt Felicity said.

Millicent took her aunt and uncle by the crooks of their arms and tugged them to a standing position. "Yum," she said. "Can't wait to try them." She half pulled, half walked them down the side walkway that led to the parking lot and to Uncle Phineas's car, yammering the whole way about how curry cookies sounded tasty to her. Her foot hit the curb and she thought she was home free. Then she heard high heels approaching. She yanked harder on her aunt and uncle.

Aunt Felicity resisted Millicent's efforts. "Millicent, what are you doing?" she asked.

"Well, well, well," a voice from behind them said. "If it isn't the Fabulous Flying Felicity."

Aunt Felicity came to a halt and she stiffened as if she'd heard a disembodied voice rising directly from the grave. Her eyes went beady.

"Look! Almost to the car," Millicent said. "A few yards more and we'll—"

"Pretty Liddy," Aunt Felicity said.

"Be there," Millicent finished weakly.

Aunt Felicity turned slowly to face Pretty Liddy, as did Uncle Phineas and Millicent. For the first time, Millicent saw what Pretty Liddy looked like. Except for her nose, which was a bit larger than most people's, Pretty Liddy seemed quite average to Millicent—dressed up and made up, but average nonetheless.

Fiona, Heinrich, and Ebi stood behind Pretty Liddy, like little fashion henchmen, while Paisley stood off to the side looking like she wanted to be somewhere else. The other Pretty Liddys lingered nearby.

"It's been a lifetime, hasn't it?" Pretty Liddy said. She took a step forward and extended her hand to Aunt Felicity.

Millicent looked closely at her. She didn't even have beard stubble.

Aunt Felicity didn't take Pretty Liddy's hand. "It has been a lifetime," Aunt Felicity replied. "A lifetime spent wandering the streets for me, far from home with no memories to call my own."

Pretty Liddy dropped her arm. She rolled her eyes as if she'd been inconvenienced. "Oh, that," she dismissed with a wave of her hand. "I heard about that."

Aunt Felicity stared at her.

"What?" Pretty Liddy asked, but Aunt Felicity didn't answer. "Oh. You think I was responsible for your disappearance?" She laughed a bit too theatrically. "Really, Felicity. What a claim," Pretty Liddy continued. "You'd have to have proof to support that preposterous allegation."

Millicent plunged her hands in her pockets, nervous that the two women were about to get into an argument. She felt a sheet of paper.

"She does have proof!" Millicent shouted. She produced the paper. Her hands shook as she unfolded it.

"Oh, little badly dressed girl," Pretty Liddy said.

Fiona giggled.

Millicent presented the sheet of paper to Pretty Liddy.

"Scribbles," Pretty Liddy said. "Nothing but scribbles."

Millicent could tell that Pretty Liddy couldn't make sense of the drawings and numbers on the paper. To Pretty Liddy, the paper could have been a page ripped from a Chinese phone book. *Good*, Millicent thought. She hoped her aunt and uncle would forgive her this time for lying. "They're calculations," she said with more than a little authority, "and they show that you were, irrefutably, the one who tampered with my aunt's cannon."

Pretty Liddy showed the sheet of paper to Fiona. "Is this true?" she asked. Fiona shrugged. She showed it to Heinrich, then to Ebi, each time asking, "Is this true?" but each time she got a shoulder shrug. Then she turned to Paisley and asked, "What do you think?"

"Millicent is pretty smart," Paisley answered. "She invents things."

"It is true," Millicent said.

Uncle Phineas winced at Pretty Liddy, but held his tongue.

"I'll show you," Millicent said. She had a plan. She hoped with her entire being it would work. Using the sheet of paper and a pen, she went into a long-winded, contrived explanation about how only someone of Pretty Liddy's height and strength could have changed the trajectory of Felicity's cannon. She threw in lots of $X$s and $Y$s and words like "fulcrum" and "velocity" and phrases like "weight to mass distribution" to make her theory sound like a reality. And, to top it off, she scrawled layers of phony calculations on the paper to make it more confusing.

Pretty Liddy watched and listened, her face growing

more contorted with each word and equation. Soon, she started turning red and wringing her hands. Finally, she exploded. "OH, STOP IT!" she shouted. "I CAN'T TAKE IT ANYMORE. ALL RIGHT, SO I DID AIM YOUR CANNON TOWARD THE TENT TOP!"

Everyone recoiled.

"I don't know what came over me," Pretty Liddy continued. "I was so jealous of you. You were so pretty. All the circus performers were pretty. I just had a big, ugly beard." Her eyes got teary. "Tilting your cannon seemed the perfect way to get rid of you."

"Her cannon?" Heinrich asked.

"Circus performers?" Ebi asked.

"A BEARD?" Fiona asked.

Aunt Felicity seemed moved by Pretty Liddy's tears. She produced a packet of tissues from her purse and offered Pretty Liddy one. "You had no need to be jealous," she said. "You had talent." Pretty Liddy took the tissue and wiped her eyes. "Anyway," Aunt Felicity continued, "what's done is done. Water under the bridge and all that. Not that you didn't cause me a great deal of pain—you did. It's simply that I'd be causing myself more pain if I didn't forgive you." She put her arm around Millicent's shoulders.

Millicent put her arm around Aunt Felicity's waist.

Uncle Phineas sidled up to the two of them, sandwiching Millicent between himself and Felicity. "My brilliant niece, yes?" he said.

Millicent put her other arm around her uncle and, for the first time in a long time, she felt like a winner.

# Thirty

Millicent sat at the edge of the Winifred T. Langley Memorial Fountain, turned so that drops of water splashed onto her face. In the morning air, they felt like cold rain; refreshing and crisp. She raised her head to catch more drops. It was almost if she were letting the fountain wash away the events of the past few weeks.

After a moment, she wiped the water off her face and looked up to see Tonisha and Juanita sheepishly approaching her. She hadn't talked to them since the election three days ago. Not because she didn't want to, but because they had kept their distance from her. She could hear them whisper as they got nearer.

"You talk first," Juanita said. She grabbed Tonisha by the elbow and urged her forward. "I'm too ashamed."

"Fine," Tonisha answered. "Don't push."

"I'll play poignant background music." Juanita raised her violin case.

"Don't you dare."

They stopped a few feet from Millicent.

"Uh, hey," Tonisha said.

Tonisha had revived her nonconformist style of not matching her headwrap to the rest of her outfit. And Juanita had evidently returned to wearing her frothy, ruffled tops. The sight of her two friends looking as they used to was enough to make Millicent want to jump off the fountain and hug them, but she contained herself.

"Hey, you two," Millicent said. "Have a seat." She patted the edge of the fountain with her hand.

"For a minute," Juanita said. "We told Mr. Pennystacker we'd show up early today to help take down—" She cut herself off, then continued in a quiet voice, "Fiona's campaign posters." She set her violin case on the edge of the fountain and sat down.

Millicent nodded. "Okay," she said.

A discomforting quiet descended on the three of them for a moment.

Tonisha inhaled sharply. "I'm . . . uh . . . I'm glad they're gone," she said.

"Me, too," Juanita said.

Millicent smiled to herself. "Remodeling sure went fast over at Pretty Liddy's Junior Fashion Academy."

"Yeah," Tonisha said, looking away. "I thought that sort of thing took longer."

The three of them sat in total silence.

Juanita tapped a rhythm on her violin case with her fingertips. "She would have made a lousy president," she said. "Well dressed, but lousy."

"Still, Fiona won. Even though ten votes is hardly a winning margin worth getting excited about," Tonisha said. "If she hadn't gone back to Pretty Liddy's Junior Fashion Academy, she'd be class president."

Once again, they were enveloped in quietness.

Tonisha flipped the pages of her poetry notebook. "Can you believe it?" she asked. "She thought a haiku is supposed to rhyme."

"Really," Juanita agreed, "or that a piano is a better instrument than a violin because a violin is a bad fashion accessory?"

"I don't know what came over us," Tonisha said.

"Me neither," Juanita said.

Though Millicent thought she'd completely forgiven her friends for deserting her, she'd *mostly* forgiven them. There remained a tiny amount of resentment in her, like old, spare change, gunky and worthless.

"You two were pretty insensitive," Millicent said.

"Mmm-hmm," Juanita mumbled.

Silence.

"And disloyal," Millicent said.

"I agree," Tonisha replied.

Silence.

"And not very nice."

"Yeah," Juanita grunted.

Silence.

"And really, pretty unlikable."

"Right," Tonisha said.

"And did I mention—"

"Okay," Tonisha said quietly. "We get it. We were bad friends."

"I don't know what came over you two," Millicent said. "It was like you became entirely different people. People I didn't know."

They sat in silence for a few more seconds.

Finally Juanita spoke. "Did you ever see that movie about the aliens? You know, the one in which Sigrid Herdman is the last person in Pinnimuk City who hasn't been possessed by aliens? What was it called?" she asked.

"*The Incursion of the Gray Matter Snatchers from Planet Zilthon*," Millicent and Tonisha said in unison.

Juanita giggled. "Yeah, that one."

Tonisha stood up suddenly. "Okay, I'm just gonna say

it. Millicent, I'm sorry. We're both sorry for being awful friends. Can you ever forgive us?"

"Can you?" Juanita emphasized.

Looking at her friends helped to make the past dissolve as if it had never happened. "What's done is done. Water under the bridge and all that," Millicent said. "I forgive you. Let's forget it ever happened." Just saying it out loud made her feel better. Her aunt had recently forgiven her worst enemy. Certainly Millicent could let the past go. She grinned at Tonisha, then Juanita. "Besides, I still got to be president, didn't I?" she added.

"By default," Tonisha said, playfully punching her shoulder.

They sat in silence again, only this time it seemed lighter and brighter, as if a huge charcoal-colored cloud had vacated the sky above their heads.

A lumbering white luxury sedan pulled up to the front of the school.

"Oh, no," Millicent said in a hushed voice. Reflexively, she tucked her tattered-tennis-shoed feet under her.

Tonisha and Juanita looked at each other, then scooted closer to Millicent.

A figure got out of the car. At first, Millicent thought

it was Fiona Dimmet, but the girl's bland hair blowing in the breeze gave her away as Paisley Slub. She made straight for the fountain with her portfolio and her laptop computer under her arms.

"What's she doing here?" Tonisha asked. She inched closer to Millicent like a lioness to a cub.

Paisley neared the fountain, and it was clear she was smiling at the trio. "Hi," she said.

"Hi, Paisley," Millicent said. "Did you forget something from last week?"

"No," Paisley said.

Juanita stood and locked her arms together across her chest. "Are you here to pick up Fiona's posters? We haven't taken them down yet."

"No," Paisley said. She looked at Tonisha and Juanita as if she wanted them to leave. "I need to talk to Millicent."

Tonisha and Juanita glanced at Millicent.

"It's okay," Millicent said.

Tonisha and Juanita gathered their things and went into the main building.

Paisley waited until they disappeared from sight. When she was satisfied they were gone, she said, "Millicent?"

"Yeah," Millicent answered.

"Is the Wunderkind Club closed to new members?" Paisley asked.

"No, never," Millicent said. "Why?"

"Even to . . . designers?"

"No," Millicent said. She couldn't help but smile.

"Great," Paisley stated quite firmly. "Because I'd be really mad if I couldn't join since I quit going to Pretty Liddy's full time. I signed up for Winifred T. Langley. I can still take extra credit classes at Pretty Liddy's. I know I'm not the smartest kid? But I can learn fast. Okay, so I forget things and sometimes I mess up. But I'm talented. Doesn't talent count?"

Millicent put her arm around Paisley and together they walked into school.

"Sure, talent counts, Paisley," Millicent said. "But there's something that counts even more."

Paisley stopped in her tracks. "Wait, don't tell me," she said. "I can guess." She concentrated for a second before saying, "Hard work counts! It's hard work, right?"

"Yes!" Millicent shouted. "Now let's get to work planning a welcome party for the Wunderkind Club's newest member."